Cookie Monsters

ALSO BY ERIKA J. KENDRICK

Squad Goals

Cookie
MONSTERS

Erika J. Kendrick

LITTLE, BROWN AND COMPANY
New York   Boston

Copyright © 2023 by Erika J. Kendrick

Cover art copyright © 2023 by Yaoyao Ma Van As.
Cover design by Jenny Kimura.
Cover copyright © 2023 by Hachette Book Group, Inc.

Hachette Book Group supports the right to free expression and the value of copyright. The purpose of copyright is to encourage writers and artists to produce the creative works that enrich our culture.

The scanning, uploading, and distribution of this book without permission is a theft of the author's intellectual property. If you would like permission to use material from the book (other than for review purposes), please contact permissions@hbgusa.com. Thank you for your support of the author's rights.

Little, Brown and Company
Hachette Book Group
1290 Avenue of the Americas, New York, NY 10104
Visit us at LBYR.com

First Edition: January 2023

Little, Brown and Company is a division of Hachette Book Group, Inc. The Little, Brown name and logo are trademarks of Hachette Book Group, Inc.

The publisher is not responsible for websites (or their content) that are not owned by the publisher.

Interior cookie vectors © Sudowoodo/Shutterstock.com

Library of Congress Cataloging-in-Publication Data

Names: Kendrick, Erika J., author. Title: Cookie monsters / Erika J. Kendrick.
Description: First edition. | New York: Little, Brown and Company, 2023. | Audience: Ages 8–12 | Summary: As twelve-year-old Brooklyn goes head-to-head against her rival to win her school's cookie-selling competition, her friends help her cope with the death of her mother and help her try to clinch the cookie queen title.
Identifiers: LCCN 2021062061 | ISBN 9780316281485 (hardcover) | ISBN 9780316281584 (ebook)
Subjects: CYAC: Cookies—Fiction. | Friendship—Fiction. | Grief—Fiction. | African Americans—Fiction.
Classification: LCC PZ7.1.K476 Co 2021 | DDC [Fic]—dc23
LC record available at https://lccn.loc.gov/2021062061

ISBNs: 978-0-316-28148-5 (hardcover), 978-0-316-28158-4 (ebook)

Printed in the United States of America

LSC-C

Printing 1, 2022

For Blondie (a.k.a. Mom), the greatest
Girl Scout troop leader and my
one and only Cookie Queen

Cookie Monsters

ONE

"**I'm going to** win it all this year!" I announce to the eighth-grade school reporter. Then, as I nervously fidget with my fingertips, I mutter under my breath, "I just have to!"

Before I can blink, lights flash from a fancy camera, and my eyeballs involuntarily dance around in their sockets. I blink a few times as the photographer sets up his next shot of me at the center of the Valentine Middle School gymnasium in front of a big display of scout cookies. The entire student body is stuffed into the bleachers, waiting for our big pep rally to begin—and they're all staring at me. I do my best to bury my nerves somewhere under my banana-and-peanut-butter-colored World Scouts Alliance uniform. *Now I'm hungry. Ugh!*

"Hey, Brooklyn!" someone says. I spin around and see the flushed face of a sixth-grade girl in a checkered romper. "Can I place an order of cookies with you?"

"Yeah, me too," says a tall girl with a bedazzled headband and matching silver bracelet cluster.

I straighten my World Scouts sash and smile as the photographer snaps our picture. "Of course you can."

The sixth grader steps forward and holds out her hand for me to shake. "We remember your big win at school last year and, well..." She grips my fingers. It doesn't seem like she's going to let go anytime soon. "Since you're the big cookie queen in these Valentine Middle School streets, we only want to buy our cookies from you."

"That's what I'm here for," I say, searching my pocket for my phone to take their orders.

The two girls look at each other and squeal, and I can't help but smile because, let's face it, I was pretty epic last year.

"I want one box of Chocolate Marvels," the girl declares, shoving her hands into her romper's deep pockets. I wait for her to continue, but she doesn't.

"That's it." She shrugs. "I'm on a super tight budget but really wanted to get my order in now before the big cookie rush starts."

"Okey dokey. I got you," I say, grinning as I take her order. Then I turn to the tall girl. "What about you?"

"On second thought," she says, "maybe I'll place my order with her." She points to the commotion happening under the basket closest to the locker rooms.

"Who?" I turn around, and that's when I see...*her*, wearing a World Scouts uniform and a slick grin. Piper Parker, the new seventh-grade transfer student, pops her hip and unravels her messy pony until her perfectly layered, shiny hair settles over her shoulder. I watch her gift Hershey's Kisses to anyone who orders scout cookies from her. She has a whole box of those delish chocolates.

"A Kiss for cookies!" Piper yells into the small crowd that's formed around her.

Ugh!

She started at Valentine midyear, right after winter break ended. The girl hasn't even been here two whole weeks, and she's not wasting any time making a name for herself.

I turn back around to face the girl who was ordering cookies from me. But both she and the other girl are gone! Then I spot them heading over to join the crowd around Piper Parker.

She glances at me and dishes out an epic hair toss. I watch her, and then she watches me, and then I watch her harder. Before I know it, we're in a real live stare-down. And I haven't been in one of those since... *never*!

"I'll place an order for a few boxes with you," I hear a soft grown-up voice say. I stop eyeball feuding with Piper to see Ms. Pepper, my homeroom teacher, swooping in to save the day. "I'll have a box of the Peanut Butter Babies and the Shortbread Shorties. And wait," she says, tapping her finger on her chin. "I should probably get a box of the Chocolate Marvels for my hubby. He just loves those things."

"Thanks, Ms. Pepper," I say, doing my best to stay focused and not check out Piper's next move.

"We're all so proud of you, and we're really looking forward to seeing you break more records this year and take home the big Valentine cookie crown."

"I really want to win the Santa Monica District title and get my hands on that grand prize."

"What's the jackpot this year?"

"I'd get to attend the big annual field trip of the World Scouts Alliance," I pipe, my smile widening. "It's a group of scouts from all around the world, and we'd help build schools for kids in need."

"Wow. That's some grand prize. We're all holding out hope for you."

Yeah. Me too.

Sarah Hines won last year. She beat me by three

stinking boxes. *Three!* She was a senior at Valentine High—but now that she's graduated, I have my eyes fixed on winning. I used to think the setup was unfair—you know, middle schoolers competing with high school kids. Seriously, some of the older girls have advantages, like CARS! Even with Sarah Hines gone, I still expect the competition to get really fierce. But I'm in it to win it, even with my biggest cheerleader and silent partner not here this year to cheer me on. I'm determined to take home that title and dedicate the grand prize to her—my mom.

The reporter snaps a few pictures of me before asking, "So, Brooklyn, how many boxes do you intend to sell this year?"

I nod at the sea of students in the bleachers. Watching the mega crowd causes my nerves to play double Dutch with my anxiety. "Enough to…to make Valentine Middle proud again!"

"Do you have a number in mind?"

"This year," I say, struggling to catch my breath, "I'm…I'm thinking five thousand boxes!"

I bend over and take a deep, long breath, and that's when I feel my troop mate, Stella Rose, grab my hand and squeeze it. "She's going to be this year's district champ," Stella Rose announces, adjusting her oyster-shell tortoise glasses and tossing her matching cashmere scarf over her scout polo.

When I look up, the rest of my troop are standing around me, blocking the reporter from snapping any more pics while I recover from this mini meltdown. I can always count on my scout squad—Stella Rose Sampson, Lyric Darby, and Luciana Lopez—to have my back.

I take a few more deep breaths and remember how amazing my friends were when I needed them most after Mom's funeral last year. We'd only known each other for a semester, but it was kismet when we met at the beginning of sixth grade. We all signed up for World Scouts and were placed in the same Sunflower troop, and, well, we just clicked.

When my breathing returns to normal and I can feel my fingertips again, I stand up straight while Lucy untangles the top row of rainbow-colored goddess braids hanging down my back. She grins at me before leaning in to explain to the reporter, "Last time, she was just two boxes away from selling a whopping one thousand of those sweet treats. This year, she's turning the volume all the way up."

I do my best to block out the crowd. I think about Mom's round, doe-eyed face and big smile, and I finish with the reporter by saying, "I want it all."

"She wants it all!" Lyric parrots me, looking the reporter square in the eye. "Did you get all that queen energy?" She pushes her big blond spiral coils over her shoulder and crosses her arms over her khaki sash that's filled with tons of creative-arts badges. I completely heart Lyric; she's the girl all the boys want to sit next to and all the girls want in their group chat.

"Okay, young people! Can I have your attention?" Principal Pootie sputters into the microphone on the podium at all the sixth, seventh, and eighth graders. "It's the second Friday of the month, and that means it's time to start our Valentine Middle Pep Rally."

I watch the Valentine Middle School HoneyBee cheerleaders get into formation on the court behind him. My squad collectively sighs as we watch Principal Pootie do his best to hype the student body. "...because we're playing Roosevelt tonight, so get your tickets for the big showdown after the rally. And finally, today begins the official Cookie Kickoff!"

My eyes dart around the gym, searching for my cheer BFF, Magic Olive Poindexter.

"To jump-start the rally, let's give a warm welcome to our very own HoneyBee cheerleaders!" Principal Pootie yells at the crowd, his spit flying through the air.

"This one's for you, B," screams Magic from the big honeybee at the center of the court. She waves at me and kicks her leg into the air with all her might. I fixate on her and my other cheer friends, Winnie and LuLu, and break into a wide smile.

At Valentine, I lead a bit of a double life. In addition to being somewhat of a cookie celebrity, I'm also one of the newest HoneyBee cheerleaders. I made the team over the summer at Planet Pom-Poms Cheer Camp, so I guess you could call me a rookie, except when it comes to the almighty cookie. Yes, I love dancing and I'm still getting better with each practice—but I'm a pro in the cookie biz. Hey, a girl's gotta have diverse interests.

Principal Pootie waves me over to the podium. I'd normally be out on that court with my squad, leading the school in all things pep, but not today.

I step up to the podium as the cheer team begins the HoneyBee signature routine with epic stunts and ends it with a dance sequence that includes a high kick line and a jump split.

The crowd howls as the cheerleaders shuffle off the court.

"We heart you, Brooklyn," LuLu sings, our tiniest flyer twirling under the basket behind Magic as Winnie rolls herself off the court in her Beedazzled wheelchair.

They blow kisses at me and wave their pink-and-gold pom-poms around their matching sparkly uniforms as they chant:

Be aggressive

B-E aggressive

B-E A-G-G-R-E-S-S-I-V-E

*That chant should be my new theme song every time
I'm in front of a crowd,* I think as I watch Principal Pootie
struggle to adjust the microphone to my height.

"And now," he says, "let's give a round of applause to
Valentine Middle's top cookie seller from last year."

Middle schoolers pound their feet against the bleachers. It sounds as if a drum section set up shop. My heartbeat twerks inside my chest to the high-speed tempo.

"Valentine's cookie champ, Brooklyn Ace!"

When Principal Pootie says my name, I look out into
the huge crowd, and something happens to my mouth: It's
suddenly Sahara Desert dry! And I'm pretty sure I can't
feel my tongue—or my teeth.

I try swallowing.

Nope, still can't feel anything.

The crowd watches me, waiting for me to say or do
something.

Awkward.

Some of those annoying public-speaking butterflies
flit around the pit of my stomach. Principal Pootie nudges
me closer to the microphone as if that's going to help
me get this party started. Mom always said to think of

everyone in their underwear. The image of the student body in their Fruit of the Looms should make me want to laugh. But it doesn't. Okay, so maybe it makes me crack a smile. That's when I double-check to see if I can feel my tongue...and yep, there it is, waiting for me to master this talking thing. I'm pretty sure my teeth are all there, too.

Whew.

Stella Rose holds up her camera to film me in front of all our sister scouts on the court while I tug on my sash, which is decorated with tons of recognition pins and leadership badges.

Then I exhale.

"Thanks, everyone!" The microphone screeches into the musty gymnasium air, and I watch as the people in the audience all wince, grabbing their ears. I look past the rafters until the kids' faces are out of my line of vision. Instead, my eyes focus on the tops of their heads.

"I'm, uh, Brooklyn Ace, and I'm, uh, pleased." No, that's not the right word. I try again. "I'm, uh, grateful..." Nope, that's not it either. "I'm uh...*honored* to be your cookie champ."

"Go, Brooklyn!" Stella Rose yells from the bleachers. She's holding her camera at just the right angle to catch the best light. She's a wiz with gadgets, and film stuff is her fave. I turn my head sideways and flash her an anxious smile.

"I, uh…"

And those are the last words I can muster before I go completely blank.

Stella Rose and Lyric begin a slow clap, and before I can say another word, the rest of the crowd has joined. I can still hear Lucy's voice over the thunderous applause. "Brooklyn! Brooklyn!" And then the whole school echoes her.

"Brook-lyn!"

"Brook-lyn!"

"Valentine Middle is very proud of you," Principal Pootie says, resting his sweaty palm on my shoulder as he nudges me away from the microphone, saving me from an afternoon of embarrassment. I'm sure it was obvious to him, and probably everyone else, too, that my speech was heading right into the disaster zone. Yep, I tanked.

"Last year's district competition was a close one," the principal says. "And this year, we'll be watching with bated breath again." Then he turns to the scouts scattered across the court and runs it all down for everyone like I didn't just bomb.

I force a tight smile, then I ease past Principal Pootie and step away from the podium as fast as I can.

"As always," he continues, "cookie season lasts for four weeks. And this year there are even greater prizes in store for the big winner." He pulls a folded paper from his shirt pocket and reads from it. "'The Valentine scout who sells the most cookies will be awarded a brand-new ten-speed bicycle and four tickets to Disneyland. The Santa Monica *District* scout who sells the most cookies will win five thousand dollars in scholarship money and a trip to London to be part of the group representing the US in the World Scouts Alliance. Their big mission this year is to…"—he flips the paper over—"'…build schools around the world for kids in need.'"

"Now, that's a grand prize, Pootie," Lyric says before she can catch herself. Dodging his pinched eyes, she stammers, "I—I mean, *Principal* Pootie."

"Yes, Lyric," he agrees, shaking his head. At this point, he's probably had enough of us. I can usually tell when that happens because he starts loosening his tie and blinking a lot, which is exactly what he's doing now when he signals the official start of cookie season.

I race through the hecticness of dismissal to catch up with my scout squad, who are all waiting for me at my locker.

"I can't believe how many new girls have joined the program this year," Lyric says as we huddle together, retelling every second of Kickoff.

"I was a mess out there. I couldn't find my rhythm at all," I say, opening my cluttered locker to shove my scout sash between my social studies and English books.

"But you did. And you were epic, as always," Lucy says, flipping her yellow-and-green hair over her cluster of design and fashion badges. "But Lyric's right; there were a ton of new faces."

Lyric sucks her teeth. "A few of them were giving you the stink eye, Brooklyn."

"Means I'm going to have to stay on top of my game. But first, I'm going to have to actually *find* my game." I shake my head in disbelief at just how tragic my speech was as I pull the red Sharpie off the magnet on the inside of my locker door. "What was my problem out there?" I scoff, drawing a line through the words COOKIE KICK-OFF on my mini dry-erase board.

"You were just nervous; it happens to the best of us," Stella Rose says, rubbing my back.

"It felt so much bigger than that," I admit. "The only thing different is..." I tap my white high-top Converse on the concrete floor. "Well..."

Lyric, Stella Rose, and Lucy circle around me and lean into our sisterhood.

"I'm sorry you're going through this," Stella Rose says, massaging her fingertips into my arm. "It's okay to feel all the feels. No matter what happens this year, you'll always be our cookie queen."

"Yeah, and you know that slinging cookies isn't exactly

13

my thing; the stage is where I shine," Lyric says. "So you can have all my cookie sales this year."

"Mine too," Lucy says. "My parentals will get the usual orders from the fam and then you can have the rest of my sales."

"Same," Stella Rose agrees. "We got you."

I turn away, inhaling one singular sniffle. "All I can say is..." I stifle a sniffle. "Wow."

"We know things are different this year, B," Lyric acknowledges. "But you always have us."

A chill rushes over me as I remember Principal Pootie announcing my name last year at the final Cookie Countdown. I remember it being harsh. I remember it being bittersweet. And then I remember why.

My mom died a week after my big victory. I hate cancer. I mean, I *really* hate cancer. For obvious reasons, I didn't have any big parties after my win. I didn't want a fancy dinner either, and I didn't feel the need to record it all for some mushy memory. Mostly, I cried. And then I cried some more. It wasn't until last summer at cheer camp that something life-changing happened. I opened up about it with some new friends, and, for the first time since Mom had died, I didn't feel numb anymore. I even went to see a cool lady therapist who knows about this kind of stuff. We only had one visit, but I remember her

14

explaining that I'm in between two stages of grief: bargaining and depression. I'm not so sure about that. I just know that I miss Mom.

Stella Rose pulls me into a hug and squeezes. "Who's our cookie queen?"

"Me," I grumble, lacking all the luster. "I'm your cookie queen."

"Not for long," a voice shrills from the small crowd forming in the hallway.

"Who said that?" Lyric challenges, stepping directly in front of me. "Because I know you're not talking to us."

I look around, but no one else is standing there— *except* us. As I shut my locker behind me, I scan the crowd until I hear *her* annoying voice.

"You know exactly who I was talking to," she says, slinking up to me. "I wouldn't be so quick to jump to the conclusion that you're going to win."

Piper Parker adjusts her sash, which is filled with tons of cool cookie badges. I try not to admire them. Instead, I focus on her eyeballs. Daggers.

She bends down to whisper into my ear, "London has fabulous shopping. It's one of my cities in heavy rotation."

Now, if I'm being honest, the girl dresses like she has a stylist on speed dial. Since she started at Valentine, her whole look has been next-level. Sometimes she'll even designate theme days on her Insta, telling her loyal entourage what to wear and exactly how to style their outfits. What's even more concerning is the way her followers fall in line and obey. Yesterday, everyone wore high-waisted distressed jeans and cuddly cropped sweaters. Hers had suede elbow patches with matching heeled booties. Yes, it was definitely ca-yoot, but hold on, it's not like I'm impressed or anything (okay, so maybe a little). Let's be clear: Going to London isn't about fashion shoots and shopping sprees. It's about joining the World Scouts Alliance and helping kids in need.

Being the good sport that I am, I force a grin and muddle through this conversation. "Welcome to the start of our big cookie season at Valentine Middle, Piper Parker."

"I hope you know I plan on taking what's mine," she declares, crossing her arms over her chest. "You, my dear, are so last year!"

I snort at her designer backpack as she slithers down the hall in pristine leather Polo sneakers that match her scout polo shirt. Her new troop gets lost in her towering shadow. I snarl at the kids walking behind them, a small entourage of seventh-grade girls—and even a few boys. They have already fallen under her spell.

Lyric stomps her chunky heels into the floor and yells

into the air, "If it's a cookie war you want, that's what you're gonna get."

"Who does she think she is?" Lucy asks, only she's not really asking. It's already become crystal clear.

"I know *exactly* who she is," I say, leaning against my locker. "She's my competition."

TWO

Later that evening, I'm sitting at the kitchen table for dinner with my dad and my grandma, Betty Jean. Dad passes me the macaroni and cheese, and when I reach for it, he yanks his hand back and laughs, causing me to laugh and then Betty Jean to laugh, too. Dad is one of my favorite people on the planet. Tall, good-looking (for an old guy), and fun—as far as parentals go. Usually, he has it all together. He's structured, prepared, and organized, but Mom's death has been pretty hard on him. Sometimes he needs a little help. That's where Betty Jean comes in.

"Betty Jean, why is my dad so silly?"

"He's always been that way, Brookie," she says, taking

the ceramic bowl of mac and cheese from Dad and passing it to me. "Can you believe that he was born giggling? The doctor couldn't believe it, but I knew right then that my son was going to be a jokester."

"Thanks for not leaving me at the hospital, Mom," Dad says, winking at her. I wink at her, too, because without Dad, I don't know what I'd do. I feel the same way about Betty Jean now that she's here with us.

Betty Jean moved in with us to help with the transition right after my mom's funeral. Once she got here, we never wanted her to leave. She said she doesn't have anywhere else she'd rather be. There's only one major rule: We can't call her *Grandma*. If we do, she'll pretend she doesn't know us. It's usually pretty funny, especially when we're standing right in front of her, trying to get her attention. She insists that she's too young to be called anybody's grandma, which is fine because *Betty Jean* fits her perfectly. She's fashionable and smart, and always fun to be around. I'm lucky, too, because she still does the grandma stuff, like baking cookies and making pies. She even sorted out the dirt in the back of our bungalow to start the tiniest garden.

"I have something pretty cool for you, kiddo," Dad says, spooning way too many lima beans onto my plate. He nods at a big white leather binder in front of me on the table.

"What's in it?" I ask, picking it up and flipping through all the pages to find tons of names and phone numbers staring back at me in the most gorgeous cursive. "I'd recognize this handwriting anywhere," I swoon. "That's Mom's writing." I turn to Dad.

"It was her binder. She called it her cookie collection. It has all of our family's and friends' information in there, including what cookies they order each year, how many boxes of each, as well as little notes about how everyone is doing."

I take my time and study the first few pages. "It's filled with history."

"That's a treasured binder, Brookie," Betty Jean says softly, her voice hovering in the air above the salad bowl.

"Now you should be all set for the start of your big phone-a-thon tonight," Dad says, smiling. "Talking to everyone was one of your mom's favorite things to do at the start of cookie season. Our family looks forward to catching up on those special calls."

"Sounds like it's about more than just buying cookies, Brookie," Betty Jean acknowledges, placing her palms over her heart.

"Let's see," Dad says, "we haven't had a good catch-up session with your aunt Leona and uncle Ted in Virginia since last year."

"I can't even remember the last time I talked to them," I admit. "I'm not sure I'd know what to say."

"They're family. It'll be a wonderful conversation. And you can find out how your big cousins are all doing."

I swallow my greens and geek, "My cousins are on that list, too?"

Dad flips through the pages, pointing at different entries. "And your godparents, your mom's old boss, and your kindergarten teacher."

"No way." My brows dance around my forehead. "Mom kept in touch with all those people?"

"They'll be over the moon to hear from you directly." Dad moves his steak around his plate but doesn't bother cutting it. "She loved every second of this. She really had a way with people, your mom."

"She was like an angel who could get inside your heart and make it wiggle to the beat of love," Betty Jean says, reaching for Dad's hand. "And you're just like her, Brookie."

I check out my reflection in the back of my spoon. "I don't see it, Betty Jean, but I'm glad you do." I put the spoon down and shrug.

Dad takes a heavy breath. "I miss her so much, especially around this time of year, when reconnecting with family was her biggest joy."

I poke my fork into the lima beans. "It's just not the same without her. That's why I made a big decision today at the pep rally."

Dad and Betty Jean lean closer to me, their curiosity piqued.

"I decided that I'm going to dedicate this entire cookie season to Mom."

"That's a beautiful gesture, kiddo," Dad says. "I'm sure she would be so proud."

I gulp down some sweet tea and wipe my mouth with my paper napkin, explaining my thought process. "See, every year, Mom was always so excited about the World Scouts Alliance's grand prize. She always said it was especially necessary to make the world a better place."

Dad tugs on his peppered goatee and thinks for a few seconds. "If I remember correctly, last year's big prize was an opportunity to work with...with..."

"With Feed the World, Dad," I say, rescuing him from his memory lapse. "The big winners got to go help organize food drives for kids in underserved countries.

"Mom was all about making a difference," I say, thinking about the disappointment in her eyes when I didn't win the district title. Sure, she tried to hide it, but I know Mom, and whenever she used to tap her right foot against the floor like she was targeting ants, we all knew she wasn't a happy camper. "She would have loved the prize this year."

"So, Mom's your motivation?" Dad asks, getting choked up.

"Yeah, Dad. She's all the inspo I need." I push my plate back, suddenly ready to hop on the phone and make some calls. "See, now I just have to win."

I grab Mom's binder and push myself from the table.

"May I be excused?"

Dad wipes his eyes with his napkin and nods. "Don't mind me. I'm just dealing with some serious allergies. The pollen count must be through the roof this year."

"Sure, Dad. If pollen count is better known as tears."

"I'm sorry." Dad fusses with the corners of his eyes, tossing the napkin and drying them with his shirtsleeve instead. "I just miss her, and when I look at you and the young lady you're becoming, I see her everywhere: in your warm smile, in that determined glint in your eyes, in your strength and perseverance. It's almost like she left the most precious piece of herself behind."

Betty Jean sniffles, and it nearly causes a ripple effect at the table. Before I unload a ton of tears, too, I turn away from memory lane and pad down the hallway with one thing on my mind.

I head into my messy bedroom and try to find a place to

set up shop and start making calls—but there's stuff *every-where*. Admittedly, I'm not the neatest twelve-year-old in the world, but lately, even I know my problem is seriously out of control. It's just that I've been so focused on cookie season prep that cleaning my bedroom—or anything else—has taken a back seat. Normally, my room is comfortably messy, but still cool. After the summer, Dad painted it crimson red and wallpapered an accent wall in a pattern of black-and-white high-rise buildings. It makes me think of New York, which is where I want to go to college. Mom always said if you fail to plan, then you plan to fail. And I'm not about that failure life. Juilliard is my plan. And then business school at Berkeley. But first, the cookie crown.

I plop down at my desk and shove the scattered papers out of my way to make room. I turn the pages of the binder and settle on calling Aunt Leona and Uncle Ted to jump-start the phone-a-thon.

I take a few deep breaths before dialing the number. It rings and rings and rings and…finally a voice peps on the other end of the line.

"Hello?"

"Uh…um, hi, Aunt Leona?" I stumble over my words at first because I'm not so sure she's going to remember me. I haven't actually talked to her in—wait, I can't even remember the last time I heard her voice. *Uh boy.*

"Yes. Is this...is this my little Brooklyn?"

Whew!

"Yes, it's me, Auntie," I say, sitting up straight in my desk chair.

"Well, what a wonderful surprise." Then she yells into the distance, "Teddy, it's little Brooklyn on the line."

"Hi, Uncle Ted," I pipe, waving my hand around in the air even though he clearly can't see me.

"How are you, little one? Well, I guess you're not so little anymore. What are you now? Seventeen?"

I laugh, remembering Aunt Leona was always just as funny as Dad. "No, I'm only twelve, Auntie."

"You mean that's not the same as seventeen? Well, in that case, you must be selling cookies for your big seventh-grade cookie competition."

"Hey, you remembered," I say, drawing a big heart around her name in the binder.

"Of course, sweetheart. Now, your mom usually makes this call, but I'm so happy to see that you're stepping into her shoes and handling your business."

"I'm trying, Auntie. You're actually my first call of the season."

"In that case, why don't we have a quick catch-up sesh and you tell me how you've been."

I cradle the phone closer to my earlobe and sigh. "I'm

doing okay, Auntie. I'm excited for cookie season, but nervous since Mom isn't here."

"You'll be a big hit; it's in your genes, sweetheart. Now, I know you've got tons of calls to make, so you can go ahead and put us down for our usual."

I scan the page to Aunt Leona's last order. "It says here that you guys bought fifty boxes of cookies last year."

"And the year before that, too. We have a system. Your uncle and I store half of them in the big freezer in the garage and then we give the other half away to the after-school program down the street, where your cousins went to school."

I jot down a few notes in the binder, updating the cookie info. "I never knew that."

"It's become our little tradition."

"Thank you, Auntie, for such a big order. I really appreciate it. I'm shooting for the district title and the grand prize."

"Oh, you're shooting for that championship ring. That's amazing, sweetheart. In that case, let's double the order from last year. I'm sure we can find a few shelters in our town that would really appreciate those snacks."

"No way! Are you serious, Auntie?"

"I just love the World Scouts, always doing good and making this planet of ours better. Now, you tell my big brother that he owes me a phone call and maybe even a visit sooner than later."

"I sure will, Auntie. And thank you for your order. It's my first big one of the season."

"Uncle Ted and I wish you nothing but success, and we're sending you our love all the way from Virginia."

"I love you, too. And Uncle Ted, of course!"

I end the call and submit the order into the Virtual Cookie app. Then I just stare at the screen. A hundred boxes sold—just like that.

Whoa!

I flip through the pages in the binder and gawk at all the big orders from last year. Mom had it all figured out. I cross my legs under my desk and slide my finger over the next name on the list: Mr. Berger, my kindergarten teacher. I read through Mom's notes and see that he ordered forty boxes of cookies last year.

Double whoa!

With Mom's magical binder and this strategic plan in place, there's absolutely no way I can fail.

THREE

The next day, I'm standing in front of my mirror, ready to recite one of Stella Rose's affirmations. She's that girl—you know, the one who can find positivity in a sea of disappointment.

I fidget with my shirtsleeve and glance at Mom's binder on my desk. "I am smart. I am capable," I say, emphasizing each word even though I'm not fully feeling it, mainly because I barely made it through the first page of Mom's big binder.

"Yes, you are, rock star," Lyric says, adjusting the sash on my scout uniform. "And starting today we are going to prove that to the cookie world with our door-to-door sales around the neighborhood. Don't worry about all the calls you still have left to make; it'll work out. Pinky swear."

I wrap my arms around her and squeeze before we all turn to bolt down the hall to the front door, where Dad is waiting with an expression that I can only describe as a big stop sign.

"I promise we won't go past Mr. Sallinger's house on the next block," I say to him when he deliberately stands in front of us, preventing us from leaving to hit up the block.

Door-to-door sales is a ritual Mom started with me. We'd venture through the neighborhood together, taking orders from all the cookie lovers. This year, I want to make the sales trek with my scout squad, *without* Dad and Betty Jean, because, let's face it, we're big girls now.

Stella Rose tries on her warmest smile and pleads, too. "And we won't cross the park either, Mr. Ace. We'll keep everything on this side of Wilshire."

"Yeah, Mr. Ace." Lyric nods at Lucy, who's holding an iPad with the Virtual Cookie app already open. "We'll keep our route limited to this four-block radius."

"I really think Betty Jean should be going with you all," Dad says, tapping his flip-flop against the hardwood. "Anything can happen. Plus," he adds, poking his head out the front door and studying the sky, "it'll be getting dark soon. What do you think, Mom?"

"I understand your concerns, Sam, but the girls are almost teenagers. They'll be all right out there on those mean streets of Santa Monica," Betty Jean says, snickering.

I loop my arm through Dad's and bat my lashes. It worked last time, when I wanted to stay up past my bedtime to watch *Hamilton*. We weren't able to get tickets to the show when it was in town, so when I found out it was going to be streaming for free, I wanted to make a dazzling night of it, complete with popcorn, ice cream, and Milk Duds. It took a few minutes, but he eventually agreed. Let's just say there was a lot of eyelash batting happening during those tense negotiations.

"We'll be fine, Dad." I can hear myself whining and the octave of my voice inching higher. "We promise." I tug on his arm and smooch his scruffy cheek before grabbing a hoodie from one of the hooks in the hallway next to my winter scarves. I'm pleading right along with the rest of my scout squad, hoping I can get tons of new orders in the little daylight we have left.

Dad watches as Betty Jean blows him a sweet air-smooch. He's definitely become stricter since Mom died. Now he's always worrying that something bad is going to happen to me. He says he already lost one love of his life and he doesn't want to lose another. But finally he says, "Okay, just a four-block radius. And then come straight home. Betty Jean and I will walk you all over to Pinkberry when you get back. You can fill us in on all the orders and update us on how everyone is doing." He sighs, getting lost in thought. "Gosh, I haven't seen some of your customers in almost a year."

"Do you girls have your sales pitch ready?" Betty Jean asks.

"I just planned on saying the same thing I said last year," I tell her. "These are my Old Faithfuls, Betty Jean. They know me, so I don't really have to say much. We already have a very established relationship." I pop the collar on my white cotton scout shirt and flash a winning smile. "And to know me is to love me."

Betty Jean wags her finger at my face and sighs as we shuffle out the front door. We slow down long enough to fix each other's uniform sashes and vests.

"See you later, alligator," I shout over my shoulder as we all dash down the street to hit up our first customer.

"In a *short* while, crocodile," Dad yells back.

"Which house is first?" Lucy asks, studying the contact sheet she made specifically for the neighborhood.

I check out the row of bungalow houses and the big apartment building down the block. "I was thinking of ringing Ms. Lancaster's bell first. She *really* loves me."

"Good choice," Stella Rose says, looking over Lucy's

shoulder at the colorful screen. She hoists her professional video camera up to her left eye. Then she steadies it.

Lucy points to her iPad screen. "Says she bought ten boxes of cookies from you last year."

"What would I do without you?" I ask Lucy, but not really expecting an answer, because I automatically assume she's fully aware of her awesomeness. She's a wiz at organization, and the girl color-codes everything.

I skip up Ms. Lancaster's porch stairs, two at a time, with Stella Rose on my heels, trying to straighten my uniform. And then I just stare at the front door, rocking back and forth on my tiptoes.

"Ring it, already," Lyric says, laughing at my pregame warm-up.

She's right. *It's now or never*, I think as I reach up and press the doorbell.

I breathe out of my nostrils like a hippopotamus. As I regain composure, the door opens and I greet the older woman standing there, still in her housecoat. "Ms. Lancaster!" She shoves her reading glasses onto the top of her head, just past her gray tendrils. I notice her squinting, so I say, "It's me. Brooklyn. Brooklyn Ace. You know, your cookie queen."

"Oh. Hi, dear," she says, stepping forward to take a

much closer look at me. "You're getting big, definitely hit a growth spurt since I saw you last."

"It's always so nice to see you, too, especially when I have delicious news."

"Well, who doesn't love delicious news?" she says, stepping forward and looking around. "As long as it's not cookies you've come to sell me."

"Well, of course it is. I *am* your cookie queen, and it *is* cookie season."

"Oh no, Brooklyn," she says with sad eyes. "I already bought my cookies for the year."

"Wh-what?" I stare at her. "What do you mean, you already bought your cookies? You always buy from me." I can feel my winning smile turning completely upside down. "I'm your—"

"Yes, my cookie queen," she finishes before I can. "But the lovely young boy who came over yesterday...well, he sold me—"

"Did you say lovely *boy*?!" I spin around on my red Converse All Stars and mouth to the girls: *Piper Parker.*

"Yes, he was a little taller than you. Blond with dimples and a really wide smile."

Lucy wraps the ends of her yellow-and-green hair around her fingers before looking back at me. I shrug, without a clue—until Ms. Lancaster says, "He was wearing a Valentine Middle varsity jacket. It was black and gold with pink stitching."

This time Lucy nods at me and asks, "What number was on the back of it?"

"I think...eleven," Ms. Lancaster answers, her eyes searching the sky for more details. "He said he was assigned to this neighborhood and that he was the only one selling over here this year."

"Logan Smith!" We all yelp.

"And you believed him?!" Lyric pipes, folding her arms over her chest. "With all due respect, Ms. Lancaster, he's working for the enemy."

"The what, dear?" Ms. Lancaster asks.

"She said he's working for the cookies," Stella Rose clarifies, nudging Lyric. "She just means that he's selling for a friend."

"Yes, I believe her name is Pippa or—" Ms. Lancaster huffs. "I'm sorry, Brooklyn. Honestly, I just wanted my cookies, but I never would've bought them from anyone besides you had I known."

"I understand, Ms. Lancaster."

"Besides, your mom usually gives me a call a week or two before the season starts to lock in my order. And since, well..."

I fight through the tight ball forming in my belly and push the words from my mouth. "Yes, I understand, Ms. Lancaster."

"When your mom died," she says, turning the volume on her voice all the way down, "I just assumed you wouldn't be selling cookies this year. It was kind of her thing."

The more Ms. Lancaster goes on about Mom, the more I feel like my insides are feasting on my organs. I'm suddenly light-headed, stepping backward to steady myself. Thank goodness Lyric is there to hold me up so I don't fall.

"She gets it, Ms. Lancaster," Lyric says before I can get any more words out.

Ms. Lancaster covers her mouth with her palms. "I'm so sorry, hon."

Her face is now wrought with concern. I stand up straight and gather myself, forcing a smile. "No worries; it isn't your fault. We'll get out of your hair and hit up Mr. Tart next door."

"Oh dear," she starts, shaking her head in a way that makes my stomach burn. "I don't think that's going to turn out so well either. I saw him talking to that same young man yesterday."

"Not Mr. Tart, too. You guys were my very first customers ever."

"I'm so sorry, Brooklyn. But I'm still rooting for you, and I'll be sure to get my cookie fix from you next time."

Lucy grabs Stella Rose and Lyric by the wrists and pulls them onto the sidewalk. They study the addresses on the mailbox and then head straight for the house on the corner, which is a total waste of time, because Mr. Tart basically ends up shooting me and my adorable smile down when he explains that he really *has* already bought cookies from Logan Smith. *Ugh.*

Minutes later, I sludge back to the sidewalk to join the others.

"I bet that girl's building a sales team to help her cover more ground," Lucy snuffles into the air.

"I'd be willing to bet Piper bribed Logan," Lyric says, crossing her arms and twisting her face into a scowl. "How else would she have gotten him to go door-to-door selling cookies for her?"

I try to shake the entire thought of Logan Smith from my head. The only thing remotely cool about him is his unibrow. Some of the kids used to make fun of him for it last year, before he became the star receiver for the Honey-Bees. I think it distinguishes him from all the other boys. Mom always used to say to find that one thing that makes you different and lean into it. I'm not sure how he's supposed to lean into his unibrow, but I'm here for it. But

36

let's be clear: Logan Smith *and* his unibrow are still on my hit list.

"Why would our star receiver be intruding on B's turf?" Lyric asks.

"Maybe he likes Piper or something," Stella Rose says, trying to make sense of it.

I scoff, "Ugh. Piper is so...so...strategic."

"Maybe that's his thing." Lucy shrugs. "Strategic girls who wear cuddly cropped sweaters."

"Well, if he does like her, first...*ew!*" I flail my arms around in the air and stomp my feet for emphasis. "And second, she's doing a good job of using it to her advantage. And if you didn't notice, it's killing my sales." I groan. "Ms. Lancaster and Mr. Tart ordered a total of fifty-one boxes from me last year. They were my biggest buyers on the block."

"B, it'll get better," Stella Rose says, erasing the footage of my slow sales day. "They're just two customers."

Lucy snorts, then says, "Not at the rate Piper Parker is raiding her turf."

"I don't know if I can do this," I admit, staring down the next block of houses filled with customers who I'm sure have already been stolen.

Lucy checks out her iPad. "Don't give up, B. According to our contact list, you still have seven more houses

37

to hit, and all of them were medium-to-big spenders with you last year."

"What's the point, guys?" I throw my hands in the air. "Piper has clearly raided my hood. And without my mom, nothing is going according to plan. She was the master-mind behind this whole thing. And now everything is already so...so different."

Instead of heading to the next house on the spread-sheet, I cross the street and trudge toward a swing in the park.

My world feels like it's closing in on me. I had no idea Mom did so much to help with my sales efforts. Why didn't she ever tell me? I already missed her so much, but now I miss her even more. How is that even possible?

I say over my shoulder, "These were my streets when Mom was here. But now *her* name is stamped all over them."

What would Mom do now that Piper has stolen my customers right out from under me? Right out from under *us*? Now I see that this was Mom's sales territory, too.

I turn to Lucy on my left and sputter, "Now she's got football jocks on her sales team."

I try to fight through the feelings of failure. But it's hard. I can't help but think that I should've gotten to my Old Faithfuls sooner, before Logan even had a chance to introduce himself.

Then I turn to Stella Rose on my right. "And they're dominating."

Mom would've seen that little trick coming. *How did I miss it?* I wonder as I check out the gray sky and the clouds that are now fighting for space up there.

I mumble to Lyric, who plops down into the swing beside me, "Like I can compete with all of that without the mighty force of my mom." I sigh into sadness. "Fareals."

We take turns huffing and puffing as the streetlights come on, darkness dancing around the setting sun.

"As if," my scout squad sulks in response.

And that's all we need to say, acknowledging that we lost today.

FOUR

"Hey, Lucy, do you like this one?" Stella Rose points to a red-and-white lace hair bow with rhinestones around the satin center on the display table.

"It's whatever," Lucy says, shrugging.

We'd decided to sneak beyond Dad's four-block radius mandate for a quick dash over to Santa Monica's outdoor mall. We needed to ease the pain of Piper Parker marking her territory all over my street. Who doesn't need a little retail therapy to soothe the soul?

"We need to stop in H&M to check out their accessories, too," I say, touching all the colorful hair stuff next to the earrings. "Then we should head back to my house. I have a lot of calls left to make."

"Okay, you heard the queen. Let's make it count, people," Lyric announces as she eyes the layout of the store. She taps her bedazzled watch with pink and gold rhinestones around the face, and we immediately get to shopping.

It's funny because we always say we're going to be in and out when we head into all the adorbs stores lining the Promenade, but the shopping bug can be brutal, especially when you have a designer in tow. And that would be Lucy. She's a designer extraordinaire. She even runs her own online boutique.

"It looks eerily similar to the one you posted on your shop last month," I offer, inspecting the row of almost identical bows in the store.

"Do you really think Anthropologie's big corporate buyers are watching Lucy's itty-bitty store?" Stella Rose asks, turning to Lyric. "I mean, it's an Etsy shop."

"I get what you're saying, but if it quacks like a duck…" Lyric flips her pony around to showcase the Lucy's Looks original holding her curls together. "And this, my dear, is what they're quacking about!"

"Cluck, cluck, cluck!" Lucy says.

"I think that's a chicken," I offer.

"Whatevs," Lucy snorts, turning her nose up at the rows of underwhelming bows.

Lyric shrugs. "Look, I'm just saying. Lucy just had the biggest sales jump of her designer career."

"The holidays did right by me," Lucy cosigns, holding the store's bow up to Lyric's pony. She twists it around in the air and then, after a few beats, places it back on the table. "It's missing the love."

"Agreed," we all say in unison.

"And even with the spike in sales," Stella Rose begins, "your parentals still haven't found out about Lucy's Looks?"

Lucy's Looks is her baby. She's been working on her shop for a whole year now. When she started, she only sold one or two items a month, but now she's selling out of her inventory almost every week.

Lucy glances down the crowded aisle and steps closer to us. "Shhh! For the sake of being out in public, let's just say I don't know what *shop* you're talking about."

She's keeping that big secret from her mom and dad, but honestly, I don't know how much longer she'll be able to hide her growing empire. Her bows are her specialty and they're *every*thing! Big bows. Tiny bows. Double-stitched and bedazzled bows. The HoneyBees even contracted with her to be their exclusive accessories vendor.

Lucy's Looks is hot right now, and it's not like it'll be slowing down anytime soon. But there was just one thing.

"How do you plan on keeping this epicness from your parents?" Stella Rose presses her.

"Yeah, you're running a whole entire store from your bedroom, the one in *their* house," Lyric says, checking the size of a denim mini with pearls stitched into the hemline. "Love." She holds it up to her waist.

"Enough about my biz; it's all about Lyric's hotness right now," Lucy says, shifting the attention away from her. "You'll sizzle in that, b-t-dubs."

I agree and toss Lyric a thumbs-up as she heads for the cash register. The truth is she'd look good in anything, and if I'm being honest, the stores should pay *her* to wear their gear. It just makes sense.

"I think I'll wear this to the big musical audition next month," Lyric says over her shoulder.

"O.M.Greatness! You're trying out for *The Wiz*?" I spout.

"Of course she is," Stella Rose says, snapping her fingers. "And you'll make the purrr-fect Dorothy!"

"Thanks, guys." Lyric blushes. "But now I just need to pick a song for the audition."

"Anything by Queen Bey and you're a shoo-in for sure," I say, looping my arm through hers.

I bonded with Lyric before anyone else in our group.

We were walking into our first troop meeting and she came right over to me, stuck out her hand, and announced that she was going to be bigger than Beyoncé. At the rate she's going, it's entirely possible. She can usually be found on somebody's stage with a ring light glowing around her naturally tanned face, a fan blowing her thick hair, and a microphone in her hand.

Lyric hands the cashier a wad of singles. "I have a few bops in mind, but none of them make my voice pop."

"Why don't you ask your mom to help you?" Lucy asks, strumming through a few graphic tees.

"I know I'd ask my mom if she was a famous singer," Stella Rose says.

I couldn't agree more. "Yeah, Lyric, she's like your very own secret weapon."

"It's even aligned with today's affirmation," Stella Rose professes, raising her hands to the heavens. "Everything I need to succeed is within my reach."

Lucy inhales a bunch of air and fans herself like she's about to faint. "I still can't believe your mom's on tour right now opening for Tre Boom."

"And they're super-duper famous," I geek.

It's true. Lyric's mom is a famous singer, and her dad is a drummer in her band. Betty Jean explained that Lyric is some kind of musical prodigy. I googled that word and, yep, I agree. Lyric's mom had a hit song a few years ago, and now she's always on the road touring. That usually means she's not around much when Lyric needs her. Lyric always says that her mom is somewhere in the world chasing fame. I'm not totally sure what that means, but I sure hope she catches it.

"I appreciate the positive vibes." Lyric looks around at us. "But I don't need my mom," she says, ending the conversation.

Later that evening, instead of Pinkberry, the girls have a giant surprise in store for me.

"I still can't believe you guys are giving up your evening to make calls with me," I say.

"Tonight is going to be amazy!" Lucy says from the middle of my bedroom. She pulls my pink-and-gold braids over my Valentine Middle tee and smiles at me. She snaps her fingers and adds, "Why wouldn't we step up to help you get through that binder and make those phone calls? I've already given this huge event a name: Brooklyn's Big Friends and Family Phone-a-thon."

"With us all pulling together to talk to your mom's contacts, we'll make a serious dent in your cookie sales."

Lyric looks into my grateful eyes, adding, "With your dad and Betty Jean making calls, too, we'll def cover way more ground."

"Yeah," Lucy says, eyeing the binder. "And Piper Parker can't get her sneaky hands on that."

I reach for the binder and hold it up to the ceiling light like it's a precious stone I found on a top-secret archaeological dig.

"Whoa! That thing's pretty big," Stella Rose says as we each take turns gawking at it in the fluorescent light.

"I know, right?" I pull it to my chest. "When I told Betty Jean that you all were going to help, she took the liberty of making copies of the pages. They're in alphabetical order, so that makes it much easier to split up."

"Who am I calling?" Lyric asks, picking up my hairbrush and holding it to her ear like a make-believe phone. She pretends to be serious, talking in an announcer's voice. "Hello there, my name is Lyric Darby, and I attend Valentine Middle with Brooklyn Ace. Unfortunately, this call is not about me. Today I'm calling you on behalf of my girl, Brooklyn. I think you might know her." Stella Rose fake-punches Lyric in the arm, and Lyric breaks into laughter.

"That wasn't bad, actually," I admit, handing off a small stack of papers. "You can take *A* through *D*. Most of them will be the Aces, from Dad's side of the family." Then I turn to Stella Rose and give her the next listings. "And you can be in charge of calling *E* through *H*. Most of your list will be the Harts, from my mom's side. They're really sweet, especially my older cousins, who are now, OMG," I flip out, doing the math in my head, "in high school!"

"Time really flies, kiddo," Dad says, easing into my messy room. He steps over piles of clothes and random stuff like there could be a bomb planted somewhere under it all. "They're going to love hearing from you all. I know I would." He finally takes a seat in the cramped space at the edge of the bed beside Stella Rose.

"I sure hope so, Mr. Ace, because I've never met any of them before, and talking to strangers isn't exactly my strong suit."

"Do you want me to take your list?" Lucy says to Stella Rose.

Stella Rose looks back at Lucy, her eyes screaming *YES!* But when she notices us all watching her, waiting for an answer, she shakes her head in a soft *no*.

"Cool." I toss her a thumbs-up before turning to Lucy, counting the next four letters in the alphabet. "You can focus on the *I* through *L* section of the binder. Most of them will be Mom's old friends from years past." I glance down at a few names. "I see Mom's old coworkers in here from the flower shop she owned and a few neighbors who've moved away." My finger stops on a name written in orange ink. "Her old college roommate, Penelope, is even in here, too."

I close the binder and sigh.

"Don't worry, Brookie," Betty Jean says, floating into the room with a tray of fresh cupcakes. She hands them off to Lucy, who grabs a red velvet one, her eyes saucering. "This is going to be a team effort. We'll rock that binder one name at a time. And your dad and I will split up the rest of them with you." She sits down and crosses arms for emphasis.

"Perf! That means you'll be calling the Ravens." I turn to the girls and explain, "They're my godfamily. My mom met them back when she was in high school. Now they have a whole family that claims me as their own—godsisters, godbrothers, godnieces…you get the point. It's a whole thing." I grin at the cuddly thought of them. "They bring me thousand-piece puzzles whenever they come to town, and we have cross-country races with everyone to see who can finish first." I laugh at the not-so-distant memory. "Mom always used to win."

I know they all must miss her. That's when it dawns on me that this phone-a-thon is going to be hard on all our family and friends, not just me. I've been so consumed with missing her that I hadn't stopped to think about how everyone else must be feeling.

When I glance at Dad, he's staring into his right palm, picking at his calluses. *This has to be hard on him, too*, I think as I pad over and rest my hand on his shoulder. He pulls me in for a snuggle and kisses my forehead.

"Mom would be so proud of you," he says. "And I don't know if I've told you, but I am, too."

"Thanks, Dad."

"And I couldn't think of better people to help you get down to business," Betty Jean says as I pull her from the bed. "Friends and family are the perfect people to practice your big pitch, Brookie. You have to let them know who you are, what you need, and how it'll benefit them."

"Gotcha," I say, more concerned with delegating office space. I point to the living room. "That's your office, Betty Jean. You can set up shop on the sofa to make your calls."

I double back to grab Dad and guide him toward the dining room. I point to the big, rectangular wooden table. "Dad, you're going to be calling from here." I hand him his list and turn back to the bedroom, where I see Lyric pretzeling her legs underneath her butt on the hanging chair and Stella Rose shoving all the clutter from my desk.

Lucy points to the kitchen. "This way I'll be closer to the snacks."

"Okay," I say, standing in the hallway, cupping my hands over my mouth. "Let's get ready to rock and roll! We've got two hours before Stella Rose has to be home to babysit Ollie."

"And I still need to show my math homework to my dad so he can check it," Lucy adds, walking out of my room, then whispering to me, "And I haven't even started it yet."

"Good grief, girl!" I balk. "You're going to get me put on punishment with you."

"No worries, I got this," she says, and heads for the kitchen, her freshly colored blue ponytail slapping against her shoulders.

Seconds later, I race through the house, checking to see that everyone is at their calling post. Once I'm satisfied, I yell out, "All right, everyone! It's time for Brooklyn's Big Friends and Family Phone-a-thon. On your mark, get set, aaannnnnd *go!*"

Before I can catch my breath, muddled voices fill the air as calls are made to people all around the country who loved my mom.

I pad into the dining room, where Dad is on the line with my godfather, Harry. He lets out a small chuckle, but it's a sad one, kind of like he did at the end of sappy movies Mom used to make him watch.

"Yeah, H, we're getting along over here, slowly finding

our way. Betty Jean is a big help—she holds down the fort—but my little kiddo keeps surprising me with her determination to keep this cookie thing going."

I pass him, smiling inside, and poke my head into the kitchen, where Lucy is gossiping with Mom's college roommate. "You got that right, Ms. Penelope. She's the most deserving scout at Valentine Middle. But let me tell you about Piper Parker. You're not going to believe this!"

I cover my mouth and snortle, moving to my bedroom to check in with Stella Rose.

"I, uh, don't know you, Mr. Hart," she sputters into the phone at my grandfather. "I, uh, just, uh, am calling to see if you want to place your order for the, uh, the, uh—"

I can't watch her in this kind of pain for one more second. I take the phone and pep, "Hi, Grandpa!"

"There's my little sweet potato." I hear his raspy voice on the other end of the line, hunkered down somewhere in South Florida.

"Grandpa!" I giggle. "I'm not so little anymore."

"You'll always be my little sweet potato. But who was that other one on the call just now?"

"That was Stella Rose. She's my troop mate. We're Sunflowers together."

"I see," he says. "Well, do me a favor and tell her that I'd like to place my order with her."

I put my hand over the phone and turn to Stella Rose. "He said you did a great job with your intro to him, and he'd love to place an order with you."

Stella Rose blushes, a shocked smile spreading across her face. "Really?"

I nod. "Yep."

She takes the phone back from me and gushes, "Thank you, Mr. Hart. I'd love to take that order from you. Give me one sec while I pull up the Virtual Cookie app."

The next two hours fly by, and in the end, I'm saying thank-you to my uncle Tommy on my dad's side, who places the final order.

I plop onto my bed, exhausted from talking to almost everyone in Mom's cookie binder, but with over five hundred boxes of cookies sold, it's the good kind of exhausted, like after a really hard cheer practice where all my muscles feel like Laffy Taffy.

I know I'm lucky to have so many people who believe in me and are rooting for me to continue Mom's legacy. And after tonight, it looks like I'm definitely on my way to boarding that plane to help kids around the world who deserve all the love and support that I already have.

I slip into my jammies and walk over to the picture of Mom and me on my dresser that was taken the last time the two of us hung out at the pumpkin patch by the Pier. It's the only thing in the room without dust on it. I stare at it and whisper-admit, "I didn't know I could love you even more." And it's true. It's like magic, because with each passing day, my heart grows bigger—and I absolutely do.

FIVE

After a big week of ups and downs with cookie sales, it's finally Friday, which means the tally for the first week of sales is going to be posted for the whole school to see. I'm having mixed feelings about it all, even though the good stuff about the weekend is staring me in the face. Weekends mean I can pretty much count on somebody having a birthday party, and that all but guarantees cake and ice cream. Then there's sleeping in late and waking up to brunch, which means pancakes or French toast for breakfast—which, c'mon, is basically dessert.

Still, today just doesn't feel like the Friday of my daydreams.

I'm in bed with my tattered notebook that's working overtime as a journal, and lying beside me are my seriously overwhelming thoughts. I feel like a station wagon has parked on top of my chest, mainly because cookie season hasn't started out exactly the way I planned, especially with the whole neighborhood missing Mom. Not only did I find out that Mom used to call everyone ahead of time to lock in their cookie orders, I also found out that Mom baked a ton of casseroles, too.

I don't know how I thought I was going to get through any of this without her, I think, when I hear a bird singing outside my window.

I look down and realize that the lined notebook paper is wet from my tears. I have no idea how long I've been crying. The ink on the page creates a smudge when I dab my bedsheet over the spots where the tears have fallen. I keep writing the letter to Mom anyway.

Dear Mom,

I'm not used to feeling this way. I mean, I always miss you every day, but this feels different. Maybe it has something to do with hearing all your friends talk about how special you were. Or maybe it was listening to family tell me so many cool stories about you always saving the day. Boy, can I relate. Betty Jean says that this is all normal after losing a loved one, but I don't know any other kid who has gone through this, so I'm not so sure how true that is. She also says that I'm feeling the pain of missing you so much because it's cookie season, our time to ride around the city, tallying our sales and winning the big Valentine title—together. But now that Piper Parker is here, things are getting complicated. Can I tell you a secret? Here goes...I don't understand why God took you away from me. Is this all my fault? Did I do something wrong? Do you think God would give me another chance to make it all right and bring you back somehow? Do you think

"Brookie," I hear Betty Jean say from the other side of the door. I unleash one long sniffle. "Are you awake? Can I come in?"

I pull the sheet up to my face and answer, "Good morning, Betty Jean. Of course you can come in."

She eases the door open and pokes her head around the stained wood before flipping the light switch. I rub my eyes and try to focus on a very blurry Betty Jean.

"I thought I heard a little mouse in here crying. That mouse shouldn't be crying at all; if anything, that mouse needs to be getting out of bed and brushing her little mouse teeth."

"I didn't see or hear a mouse," I offer, looking around the dirty stack of clothes on the floor next to my bed. "Nope, no mouse in sight."

"Well, in that case, it must've been my Brookie shedding a few morning tears," she whispers as she tiptoes past my desk to the side of my bed. "What's happening this morning that's got you stuck in a rug like a bug with your feelings?"

I shrug, fighting the urge to hide under my comforter. I hate it when I feel like I'm being a baby. Plus I don't want Betty Jean worrying about me, especially since she hasn't even been here a full year yet. I don't want to give her a reason to leave; there's no way I could bear losing her, too.

"I wasn't crying. Really," I say, fixing my face to smile through my little white lie. I shove my notebook under the pillow and hop out of bed.

"Today's a big day for you, Brookie. That wouldn't have anything to do with you feeling all the feels, now, would it?"

I shuffle through the clothes in my closet and pull out my red tracksuit with the singular white stripe down the sides of the jacket and the pants. "Every day is a big day in the seventh grade, Betty Jean."

She leans back on my bed and crosses her legs. Her painted toes dangle in the air. "Brooklyn Aerial Ace, you know what I mean."

I pretend not to have any idea.

"I just want to know how my Brookie is handling all the pressure."

I lean against the wall and profess, "I'm doing just fine, Betty Jean. Dad always tells me to treat the big days like the little days and don't make any of it mean anything."

"But this *does* mean something to you, sweetheart—and that's okay. It's all about how you choose to deal with it. If I were you, I'd be having some anxiety and probably some doubts about my success this week after Piper Parker put a monkey wrench in my sales goals."

"You mean she stole my Old Faithfuls!"

I can feel Betty Jean watching me bury my head deeper into the hood of my jacket. I peek out and watch her ease herself from the bed and head toward the door. Before she ducks out, I sneak one big snuggle into her. She sighs, sliding her arm around me and kissing my cheek. "I'm always here if you want to talk about your feelings. They're yours and they matter."

Before she leaves the room, she nods at the picture

of Mom and me on my dresser and says, "She sure was
something special."

Later that day, I stare at a different photo of Mom that's
taped to the inside of my locker. It was taken two years
ago at Easter. She dressed up like a bunny and hopped
around the neighborhood, giving out organic fruit. Come
to think of it, she gave Mr. Tart a casserole that day, too.

"Listen, B, you have to look at the big picture; we're just
getting started with this thing," Lyric says, applying her glittery gloss to perfection, never looking in the mirror.

I blow an air-kiss to Mom before turning to face the
girls. We agreed that we'd all walk over to Principal Pootie's office after lunch to check out the rankings for the
cookie tally. In order to do that, I have to actually make it
down the hall and around the corner without vomiting all
over my Vans. My stomach is in knots, and it doesn't help
that Lucy, Lyric, and Stella Rose are looking at me with
what I can only call pity.

Stella Rose unzips my jacket and pulls out my braids.
"She's right. It's only the first week."

I fidget with the ends of my hair as Lyric inspects my
colorful cornrows, which are sectioned off horizontally.
"This symmetry is stunning."

"Thanks," I say, only half smiling.

Lucy loops her arm through mine, and the ruffles on the sleeve of her flirty blouse get mussed somewhere underneath my armpit. Without giving it a second thought, she steps back and smooths out the pleats on her purple mini. "Listen, B, you've gotta remember that we have three more weeks to go. And in the world of cookie sales, that's an eternity."

"Look," Lyric starts, staring me right between my eyeballs. "You had a topsy-turvy week. But we have to agree that the phone-a-thon is going to cause ripples in the overall tally."

"Have some faith in the power of your loved ones," Stella Rose says, swiping through her phone until she lands on her fave page. "Today's affirmation is 'Everything that is happening is only for the highest good of me.'" She grabs one of my hands, and Lyric tosses her arm over my other shoulder. When I don't budge, Stella Rose lifts my head from the locker. After a few seconds, I give in.

"Okay, okay, it's all for the highest good," I say, placing my fingers over Mom's picture. I close my locker and turn to face the music. "Now. Let's go see the dumb list."

We make the long trek down the hall and round the corner in the opposite direction of Mr. Reynolds's English class. And then ... at the end of the hallway, there it is.

VALENTINE MIDDLE
WORLD SCOUTS COOKIE SALES
WEEK 1 RANKINGS

It's hanging on the bulletin board beside Principal Pootie's office door in black cutout letters.

"I don't know if I can look," I say, tugging on Lyric's satin jacket, which is covered in pink-and-black animal print.

She tucks her blond curls behind her stacked cuff earrings. "Of course you can do this," she says, stomping her suede bootie into the floor.

Stella Rose pulls her hands out of the pockets of her cutoff shorts. "You were born for it." She digs into her backpack and pulls out her camera. "Cookie sales are in your blood."

"But it might not even be as bad as you think. Let's look and see," Lyric says, poking me in my arm with her blingy press-on nail.

I tread slowly up to the sheet of paper that's taped to the center of the board. As I get closer, the singular page appears to get smaller and smaller and...

The names are mushed together.

My heart pounds and my palms are sweaty. I wring them out before swiping them down the sides of my joggers. And then—a thought pops into my head. What if I didn't even make the list at all? Principal Pootie posts only the top five. What if I was number fifteen or even number fifty and not good enough for a singular mention? I'm not familiar with this overwhelming feeling, that same one I felt at the podium.

Uh-oh.

I try to move, but I'm completely frozen.

"Don't worry, B, I'll look at the list for you and report back," Stella Rose offers, putting her camera away while Lyric fans me with one of her neon notebooks.

Lucy holds up my shoulders. "You're okay, just snap out of it."

"I don't think she can just snap out of it," Stella Rose tries to explain to Lucy. "It's not always that easy."

"I just meant...well," Lucy says, turning to me to finish. "You got this. Sooo, let's go get this!"

Maybe my scout squad is right. I try doing everything in my power to pull myself together: a few deep breaths and a fake smile should do it.

I center myself before walking right up to the list—that's what Mom would want.

Stella Rose and Lyric are on either side of me, and Lucy positions herself behind me.

"I'm fine. Really," I say, focusing my eyes and shaking my shoulders like a heavyweight boxer before a big fight.

I run my fingers down the names on the list in search of mine. I stop beside the number...FIVE. "I CAME IN FIFTH!" I screech.

"You came in fifth," Lyric parrots me. "She came in fifth." She turns the notebook on herself and fans her face feverishly. "Fifth is good," she says, her voice starting to quiver. "Really, it is...good."

"Guys, it is," Stella Rose declares. "Two minutes ago, she was afraid to even look at the list. And now her name is right there—on the list!"

"Mr. Tart, Ms. Lancaster, and the rest of the block really set us back," Lucy says, studying the contact spreadsheet on her iPad. But it was the friends and family phone-a-thon that saved us."

"And of course, Piper Parker is number one," I mutter, still staring at the list as if my laser glare will somehow change the rankings. Even though I want to have a positive attitude, it's a total struggle right now. I sulk deeper into my funk. "She took the top spot."

"Facts!" Piper's voice perks into my right ear. When I turn around, I see her arms folded over her houndstooth blazer. She unfolds them to trace her hand in the air around my face. Then she shoves it into the pocket of her leather joggers before sucking her teeth. "You didn't think you were going to beat me, did you?" She laughs at her own words. "Just because I'm new here doesn't mean I'm working from a disadvantage. You're just not what's hot anymore." Piper Parker sucks her teeth again and rolls her eyeballs around in her head before spinning to walk away. Her fingers explode into the air as she snakes down the hall. "In your face, Brooklyn Ace!"

"Ew!" Lucy rages at the back of Piper's springy high-lighted ponytail. "She makes my stomach churn!"

Lyric pops a piece of grape bubble gum into her mouth and chews hard. "That's because," she starts, but stops to blow a bubble, "Piper Parker doesn't have any manners. She needs some good home training."

But Piper doesn't bother to turn around and defend herself. Instead, she disappears around the corner and into a world where she's the highest achiever.

"It's only the first week," Lyric consoles me, shaking her leg, which is smooshed into a pair of shiny black bicycle pants. "We just gotta step up our game and get you to the top of that list. Where else can we go sell our cute little hearts out?"

I take a long, deep breath, and then it hits me. "Montana Avenue!"

Montana Ave is on the side of town with all the fancy shops and the cute upscale eateries. You know, the side of town where the people are spending their coin.

"Yes!" Lucy says, already digging around for data on the neighborhood.

"Love," Lyric cosigns. "Expanding our sales territory is a brillz idea. I'm all for racking up more sales on the ritzy side of town. Show me the money!"

Stella Rose knits her brows. "I sure hope we have better luck with the big houses."

I grab her hand and squeeze for emphasis. "There's only one way to find out."

SIX

The next twenty-four hours were spent in our group chat texting back and forth about our new, detailed Montana Avenue cookie plan. We even enlisted Betty Jean to rock with us, and she's driving us down the crowded Santa Monica street filled with eateries and trendy shops.

"We're here, girls," Betty Jean says, scanning the back seat. She pulls over right in front of Peet's Coffee in her sweet ride, a hot-pink Cadillac convertible. That's right, my grandmother drives the hottest car in town. She even slows down to wave at all the lookie-loos whenever she makes her way to the cleaners or the market.

When she shuts off the car, my scout squad hops out, ready for our second round of door-to-door sales.

"I think it's a good idea that my mini-moguls picked this neighborhood," Betty Jean says, sliding on her sunnies and checking herself out in the rearview as two middle-aged women with strollers that look like Transformers take pictures of Betty Jean's Caddy.

"I don't know why I didn't think of it sooner. It's so family-friendly," I explain, watching Betty Jean slide from the car and join us.

"And the houses are huge," Stella Rose says.

"Exactly." I say, pointing at the imaginary board like I do every time I explain probability to Lucy after Mr. Chang's math class. "And big houses have kids, and kids love cookies, so I have high hopes for Montana Ave."

Betty Jean puts her hand on my shoulder and glances at me. "Do you know what you're going to say when your prospective customers open the door? I know I've said it before, but that initial sales pitch is very important."

"I'm just going to say that I'm the cookie queen. That should do it." I pull my sash over my head and inspect my scout uniform. "Plus this outfit will say the rest, Betty Jean."

"Yes, Brookie, but these are new customers, and you don't already have a relationship established. It's very important that you all have your pitch down. How about we do a practice run before you knock on that first door." She tosses her Hello Gorgeous tote over her shoulder and rubs her hands together.

"We got this, Betty Jean." I tie the pristine white shoestrings on my Vans. "Besides, who wouldn't want to buy cookies from us?" I loop my arm through Stella Rose's, and we stand on the corner and make silly poses until Betty Jean laughs, too.

Lucy pulls out her iPad. "We're in it to win it today, Betty Jean."

"The universe is on our side," Stella Rose affirms.

Lyric fiddles with my hair until she thinks it's perfect. Then she gives us each a Lyric Darby once-over and finally approves. "The peeps over here won't know what hit 'em today."

"We thought you could use a little extra ammo, so while we were in Chang's class," Stella Rose says, a sly grin sneaking across her face, "we started another secret group chat."

Lucy crosses her arms over her chest. "Let's be clear here; this was not my idea. None of it."

"What?" I ask as Lyric slides out of my way to reveal four misfit band members lurking behind a big tree. They're dressed in their Valentine band uniforms with their instruments in their arms.

"It's the band!" I yelp. "Well, some of them."

"I enlisted them to help create a vibe for us today. They're here to pump up the volume!"

I watch a kid with a mullet holding a tambourine. He's talking to another kid with choppy bangs and flooded pants who's gripping his clarinet for dear life.

Lucy eyes the boy with the cymbals. He snorts as he shoves his horn-rimmed glasses with the tape holding them together up his nose.

"It was last-minute," Lyric explains. "I took what I could get."

"I think it's cool," I say as a purple SUV pulls over and two HoneyBee cheerleaders hop out.

"OMG! It's Magic!" I yell, running over to clobber her with hugs and high fives. "What are you doing here?" I turn around, enthusiastically waving at Winnie, who's being helped out of the truck and into her wheelchair by LuLu.

"The StumbleBees came to cheer you on," Magic announces. She chomps on a Twizzler and then offers me her last one. I happily accept; I know how much her candy vines mean to her. She swallows and grins, waving her pink-and-gold poms around my face. I giggle when she yells, "Gooo, Brooklyn!"

Winnie rolls up to me and says, "When Lyric mentioned that you needed backup, we just had to be here."

"We're your biggest cheerleaders," LuLu says, until Lyric clears her throat so loud that LuLu's brows shoot into her forehead.

"Okay, okay. We're *some* of your biggest cheerleaders."

Lyric settles and smiles. "Let's keep it cute."

The Stumbles get in line with the band and wait for their cue.

Betty Jean smooches my forehead and whispers into my ear, "Looks like you've got it all handled, Brookie. I wouldn't change a thing." She grins at all my girls. "Ring me when you're done; I'll be at Williams-Sonoma."

We all wave to Betty Jean and turn to face the long row of monster houses on Fourteenth Street.

"Here we go," Stella Rose says, and marches right up the porch to the front door on the house with the white siding. She rings the doorbell and knocks a few times, too. "Time to sell some cookies!"

"You ready, B?" Lyric asks, shaking my shoulders.

I straighten a few pins on my sash and paste on my champion smile. "Ready as I'll ever be."

"Perf!" she yells as the front door swings open and a really tall woman with thick eyeglasses and a fuzzy wig appears.

Lyric cues the HoneyBees and the band. They start a dance routine as the band clanks their instruments together in a really sad attempt at our school song.

"Hi," I say, extending my hand. But the woman just looks at me, waiting for me to finish my sentence, never bothering to shake. "Hi. Um...well, um..."

"Can I help you with something?"

"Well," I continue, "I attend Valentine Middle School, and uh...well, today—well, not just today but..." I swallow hard and try to finish. "What I'm trying to say is that I'm selling—"

The woman doesn't even let me finish my sentence before she mutters, "Don't care. Not interested," and slams the door in my face. My eyes bug out of my head because, well, she slammed the door *in my face*!

Stella Rose cues the band to stop the music. The dancers freeze in the middle of a grapevine when the cymbals clank together.

"Uh-uh, wait a minute," Lyric snaps, raising her hand to beat down the door. "Did that lady just have the nerve to—"

"Let it go, L-Boogie," Stella Rose says. "Let's just hit the next house. Don't let it get to you."

"Besides, did you get a look at that rat's nest on top of her head?" Lucy chuckles, choking on her own dark humor. "I mean, we can't take her seriously!"

We all giggle when Lyric says, "We should've slipped her Betty Jean's card for an emergency appointment at Betty Jean's beauty bar, Curls and Pearls."

Lucy deletes the order form on her iPad, and we press on as she pulls up the next one, which matches the address on the Mediterranean house with the orange trim. Stella Rose nods at the band again, and the girl with the drums starts a new beat. The dancers twirl around behind us as we walk a few paces to the latched gate and open it like we belong there.

"I don't know what happened to me back there," I admit. "Like for real, I couldn't find my words."

"No worries, you got this," Stella Rose says with a degree of confidence that I seem to be missing. Then she rings the bell. "Just breathe, B. You're doing great."

Magic yells out, "Gooo, Brooklyn!" and then the other two Stumbles yell it, too.

I wink at my girls and clear my throat. I center myself and inhale until my belly can't take in any more air, waiting patiently for someone to come to the door.

"Who is it?" a gruff man asks, not bothering to open the door—at all.

"It's Brooklyn Ace," I say, with no further explanation.

"Do I know you?"

"Uh...no." I turn to Lyric and shrug, but she grabs my shoulders and steadies me. So I continue with my introduction. "Uh, sir, I'm a scout at, at...uh—"

Valentine Middle, Lyric mouths at me.

72

"Valentine Middle, sir, and I was wondering if—"

"Go away or I'm calling the cops."

The cops?!

Lyric shoves me out of the way and screeches into the screen door, "Calling the cops on a bunch of scouts? What do you think we're going to do, start a campfire on your front lawn and make s'mores?"

"You've got five seconds to get off my property!" he threatens, unbothered by Lyric's preteen hostility.

Stella Rose, who has a growing fear of getting into any kind of trouble, grabs my elbow and yanks me off his steps. She waves her hands over themselves, cueing the band to abort the mission. "We gotta get out of here," she yells as she pulls me down the block.

"What is wrong with me today?" I sulk, shoving my hands into my hips as I hightail it down the street behind her.

"It's not you, it's them," Lucy says. "I think they all got up on the wrong side of the bed."

"But this is supposed to be the side of town with all the '*op-por-tu-ni-ty*,'" I complain, making air quotes.

Stella Rose scratches her head. "I don't get it."

"I hear ya, sister," Lyric says, tapping her red Converse on the pavement.

"We can't give up now." Stella Rose coaxes us to keep going. "Let's try the next house."

"I'm getting hangry," Lucy moans, facing Montana Avenue. "And this uniform is making me itch."

"We have to stay focused," Stella Rose says, tugging me toward the next white stucco house. She waves her arms around, and the band begins another drab song while the StumbleBees move to their disjointed beat.

Stella Rose encourages the band before turning back to me. "Let's give this house a try." She raps on the front door and then rings the bell. "This is the one; I can feel it."

But it isn't. And neither are the next three! Our Montana Avenue adventure is a total bust, and all I can think about now is froyo with Fruity Pebbles sprinkles.

"I'm going to Pinkberry," I say, slogging off the last and final porch on the block.

"Maybe it's just not our day." Stella Rose shrugs as the band and the cheerleaders march down the street, dancing to the dismal beat behind us. "We can take a break and then try the other side of the block."

"I think I'm done for the day," I relent, passing the houses that turned me down. "This is how it feels to be defeated. Again."

And then the inevitable happens. One by one, tears prick my eyes, and when I look up, the trees dotting the sidewalk feel like they're closing in on me. I can't stop it...

and I can't seem to catch my breath either. I know this feeling—it's the one I used to get right after Mom died.

I try hiding my eyes, but Lyric spies the angst. "Oh, B, don't cry. Please don't cry."

"No, honey, it's not worth it," Lucy says, shaking her head.

"But to her it is," Magic soothes, trying to explain so Lucy understands.

"Sometimes…sometimes I can't stop the world from spinning," I admit. "I know that sounds dumb, but—"

Stella Rose reaches for my hand. "It's not dumb at all. It happened to my big cousin. She would tell me how the room would start to feel like it was closing in on her and spinning at the same time."

LuLu talks with her hands, her pom-poms bristling in the wind. "And I know other kids who have experienced the same thing. It's more common than you'd think."

"That's deep," Lucy says. "I'd totally freak."

"Lucy!" Lyric yelps at her. "We talked about this. Lead with your heart and try being a little more sensitive."

"It could happen to anyone, girl," Winnie says, rolling back and forth on the concrete beside the willow tree. She gives Lucy a serious side-eye. "It could even happen to you one day."

Lucy shrugs, and then she finally says, "Sorry."

Lyric high-fives Lucy before turning to me. I watch her dig into her messenger bag until she pulls out a wad of tissues and passes it to me.

"But what if I'm not good enough without her?" I whisper.

"You mean to win the Valentine Middle crown?" LuLu asks, folding her arms over her chest.

Stella Rose's voice softens before she clarifies, "I think she means in life. What if she's not good enough…like, period." She laces her fingers with mine. "It's not the same with Betty Jean, huh?"

"There's nothing like a mother," Lyric says into the air, at no one in particular. She fluffs her curls and avoids eye contact.

Lucy moves one of my braids out of my face and smiles at me. I notice her eyes for the first time—serious and sensitive now. "Let's talk solutions. Have you been journaling?"

When I nod, Magic steps closer to me, leaning into my ear to ask, "What about seeing someone again? You know, like we talked about at cheer camp last summer?"

"I didn't know you were seeing someone. Like a therapist?" Stella Rose asks, completely clueless that Magic was trying to keep it on the low.

"Dr. Simone," I admit to everyone. "But I only saw her once. Then I stopped." When Stella Rose's brows dip into her forehead, I explain. "I didn't really like talking to a stranger about my mom being gone. The whole sitch was just kinda weird." I lean against a tree, surprisingly not feeling weird talking about life and death stuff with them.

"I'd totally be down to be your therapy support if you want," Stella Rose offers.

"Me too," Lucy agrees.

Lyric shrugs. "And I'm not the biggest fan of counselors, mainly because I always feel like they try to get all up in my business, but if that's what you need, I'm here for it."

"And you know I already promised to be your therapy buddy," Magic says, gleaming at me and crossing her arms over her Valentine cheer uni.

"Are you guys serious?" I ask, shocked at all the support. I stop kicking at the grass beneath my sneaks.

"Sometimes these things take time, B," Stella Rose encourages, tossing her periwinkle scarf around her neck for emphasis. "And we're twelve; we've got time."

Winnie rolls her chair straight up to me and adds, "My old babysitter used to see a counselor. She went every week for, like, a year."

"Why?" I ask.

"She was dealing with some anxiety stuff, and she felt

down a lot. She just couldn't shake it off without some extra support."

"Did it help?"

"She said it did, but it took time."

I check out my shoestring again and shrug. "I'll think about it and let you guys know."

"While you're figuring that out, we're still here for you," Lyric says. "We're not professionals, but we're always here to listen—as friends. Real friends. Well, maybe not Lucy with the listening part; we all know how impatient she can be."

"I'm just not really into processing feelings, that's all," she explains. "And maybe I could work on my patience for certain situations."

"Like that time Stella Rose's cat, Bugsy, got sick and died," Lyric reminds us. Everyone laughs, remembering the story about the infamous dead cat.

"And Lucy kept telling her to just get a new one at the shelter," I add, snuffing a giggle.

Lyric shakes her head in disbelief. "She honestly didn't understand that Stella Rose couldn't just replace Bugsy and suddenly feel better."

"But it was nice of you to take me to the adoption fair, though." Stella Rose nudges Lucy. "You didn't have to do that."

"As long as I didn't have to hear about Bugsy's final hours again," Lucy half jokes.

The girls pull me from the tree, and we head down the street toward Pinkberry. I check each of them out and remember what Betty Jean always says: *Everybody brings something different to the table.*

As we approach Montana Ave, I'm finally starting to feel better—that is, until Lucy brings it back full circle and warns, "You better get your head in the game because it doesn't look like Piper Parker is going to ease up anytime soon."

I shudder at the thought.

SEVEN

A few days later, I muster up the courage to finally go to my second therapy appointment ever. It helps that I'm not alone on the big day, because Magic is with me. I told Betty Jean that we had it covered, so she said she'd be across the street at the Whole Foods, grabbing a few things during my hour-long appointment.

I turn to Magic and fumble with my thumbs, my nerves creeping up on me as I wait for Dr. Simone.

"I've never been to a therapist before, but I can go inside with you if you want. I can sit in a corner and read one of her mags while you talk through all your stuff." Magic leans closer and adds, "That way you don't have to be alone."

When we met over the summer, we became fast friends. We talked to each other about some of the stuff we were afraid of and other stuff we were conquering, and then we laughed about everything in between. Magic is one of those special humans who always feel like a warm hug. So, when I told her about missing my mom and struggling to deal with it, she promised that if I ever went to talk to someone about it, she'd be right by my side. I decided to take her up on her offer, not because my scout squad wouldn't be cool. It's just that I'm really feeling the warm-hug vibe today.

"I think I'm strong enough to manage," I say back to her. "Hopefully."

She smiles and shrugs. "I'm right here if you change your mind. Just a holler away. A stone's throw. A skip and a jump. A—"

I hold off laughing long enough to stop her. "Thank you."

"Brooklyn, you can come in now," a soft but firm voice says over our giggles.

I turn to Magic and fan myself, my eyeballs bulging from their sockets.

Magic pats my shoulder. "I'll be right here. Waiting for you."

She pushes my butt out of the seat and gives me a gentle nudge. "Now, go handle your business and you can tell me all about it at Pinkberry over mango froyo. My treat."

I grin at Magic and turn to walk into the office, which reminds me of a sophisticated living room. I look around and take a seat on the green velvety sofa across from Dr. Simone's sleek armchair. She sits down and grabs the clipboard from the end table next to her.

The glass desk in the corner of the room sits in front of a big bay window with long taupe curtains that brush against the floor. I notice this because Mom really had a thing for window treatments. She always said they were the ultimate decoration, the eyes of a room. Then I sigh, mostly because Mom would've approved of Dr. Simone's taupe eyes.

"How've you been, Brooklyn? It's been quite a few months since I saw you last," she says, glancing through her notes on the clipboard.

"Fine," I say, shrugging. "I guess, yeah...I've been... fine."

She shifts in her seat and then leans closer to me. "Why don't you tell me what brought you here."

"Betty Jean brought me here. She's grabbing a few things at the market. But then she'll probs sneak into Sephora. She loves her some Sephora."

"Not who, but what." She smiles. "*Why* are you here today?"

I look past her and lose myself in the grayish-blue wall

that's facing me. After a few minutes, I say honestly, "Dad and Betty Jean thought it was a good idea." Then I think for a sec. "And so did Lucy, Lyric, Stella Rose, and Magic. Plus the Stumbles, too."

"And why is that?"

I know where she's going with this line of questioning, but I'm not really ready to open up just yet. I need a few introductory questions; my butt is still getting adjusted to the sofa cushions. I shift around in my seat and cross my legs to mirror hers.

"So...how's school been going?" she asks, picking up on my hesitancy.

I smile back at her, remembering my first visit here. She tried to make me feel at ease, and I appreciate that, but not enough to keep my other appointments.

"School is...well, school's been...let me think," I stammer, trying to figure out exactly how I feel. The truth is that I normally really like school, but lately it's been a struggle to get through the long days when I'm not with my scout squad or the cheer crew. I guess I should just tell her that, but I don't want her to think I'm a wuss. Then there's the fact that I still don't really want to talk to a stranger about Mom, not even to one Dad is paying his good, hard-earned money to listen to me.

"Brooklyn, I know it's hard to open up to someone

you don't really know and to tell them how you're doing. That's totally understandable—if that's even how you're feeling."

My eyes widen as I fumble with the elastic around the end of my jacket sleeve. "Yeah, maybe that's exactly how I'm feeling."

"I'd probably feel the same way if I were you," she says, putting the clipboard down. She looks at the door and then asks, "Is that one of your friends in the waiting room?"

I nod and grin. "That's Magic." I glance at the door, too, before boasting, "She's one of my besties."

"And she came to support you today. You're a lucky girl." She picks up the clipboard again. "Why don't you tell me about her."

"Well, let's see," I begin. "I met her at cheer camp over the summer when we were put in the same group. She's really sweet and funny, and she's easy to be around."

I sit back in the sofa and fold my arms across my chest like that time I explained TikTok to Betty Jean.

"I like her already."

I nod at her taupe window treatments. "Same."

"You can never have too many friends who make you feel valued," Dr. Simone says, scribbling ferociously on her clipboard. That's when I notice that her red lipstick matches her red bow tie. I scan her outfit, realizing that she's wearing red-and-gold sneakers, too. Her coiled Afro is my favorite part of her vibe. *She'd fit in perfectly with my scout squad*, I think.

"It's okay to be scared, you know. Talking about your feelings isn't always easy. But I'm here to help with that. And whatever it is that's challenging for you, it's my job to help you get through it."

"Winnie and I were talking about her old babysitter being in counseling. One of the things she said was that she learned helpful tools. She said if I give this a chance, you'll teach me tools, too."

"I can definitely do that."

"Well." I stroke the bottom of my chin like Dad does whenever he's going over the weekly household budget. "What would you tell Stella Rose to do about getting tongue-tied whenever it's her turn to read aloud in English class? Or when her heart starts racing really fast and her palms get all sweaty because she can't find her words?"

"Well, I'd tell *Stella Rose* that those are some pretty real symptoms and that a lot of kids her age go through that. I'd also tell her that it's perfectly okay to not be okay."

"Humph." I look at the door, then down at my hands, which are still a little shaky, remembering when I couldn't find my words at the Cookie Kickoff. "I'm sure she'd love to hear that."

"I find that it helps to share with children that they're not alone in whatever it is that they're going through. When we don't talk about how we're truly feeling, it's easy to think we're all by ourselves out here."

"Uh-huh. I see." I tap my foot on the floor and lean in—just a little.

"I'd also tell her that it sounds like what she's experiencing could possibly be anxiety. Of course, I'd need to do a full assessment before making that diagnosis."

"Of course," I say back to her.

"But I'd teach her a few coping strategies to help those symptoms pass."

I prop my elbow against the arm of the sofa and sit quietly. Dr. Simone doesn't ask any more questions for a few minutes. I appreciate the break, but after I gather my racing thoughts, I decide to try to open up.

"It's hard sometimes." I watch the wind blow the curtains around the parquet floor. "School."

"And why is that?" she asks, picking up the conversation like she never left.

"I dunno. I usually don't have issues in that area. I'm ranked top in my class. Betty Jean says I'm competitive, but lately, some stuff has been going on that has me getting down on myself."

"Do you want to talk about some of it? I'm all ears

if you do. And this is a safe space with absolutely no judgment."

I take one long breath and deep-dive into the whole story about Piper Parker transferring to Valentine Middle and stealing my spot. I even share with Dr. Simone how I came in fifth on Friday's cookie tally and how everyone laughed at me—at least I think they did. Then I tell her how I don't have any idea how I'm going to beat Piper and reclaim my title, espesh after two failed door-to-door attempts.

"That's a lot to deal with, Brooklyn," Dr. Simone says, jotting down the last few words onto the paper.

"I know, right?!" I suck my teeth and fold my arms across my chest. "I'm not used to losing. And I'm definitely not used to tanking onstage or being tongue-tied or out of breath or..." I stop, realizing I've already said more than I wanted.

"How have you been handling it?" she asks, softly.

I swipe at my cheeks, realizing that they're wet. "I don't know why I'm starting to cry."

"I imagine you're crying because it's a big deal to be disappointed. And to feel like people are laughing at you. That's nothing to take lightly. And tears are okay; you never have to be ashamed to release them, especially in here."

I shrug again and wipe my face with my jacket sleeve. "I guess I handle it by writing sometimes."

"You mean in a journal? Or a diary?"

I shake my head. "I wrote a letter. One stupid letter."

Dr. Simone reaches for the tissue box on her desk. When she hands it to me, I start to cry even harder. She lets me sob in her office until I don't really feel like I have any tears left.

She gives me a cool felt pen and a new red notebook with empty pages.

"You can write as many letters in that as you want—to anyone you want."

I turn to the first page and scribble something across the lined paper. Then I turn it around so she can see. She reads it aloud.

" 'Why did God take my mom away?' "

EIGHT

That night, I barely sleep. Too much stuff on my mind after my time with Dr. Simone, leaving my brain both cluttered and laser-focused at the same time. I'm up thinking about Mom one minute and Piper Parker the next. I don't even know Piper Parker, but I'm taking her attack on my cookie kingdom personally.

I keep asking myself, *What would Mom do?* I've already missed a few key things, like checking in with my old customers ahead of time. But I try to get my head back in the game. Today is a big sales day with the girls, and if we pull it off, it could really position me for a cookie comeback.

My desk is still atrocious, I think as I stare at it with no idea how to start sorting the clutter. So I just shuffle math worksheets from one side of my study space to the other.

There. That's better.

Dad pokes his freshly shaved head into my chaos. "You know you missed chore day. This bedroom should've been at the top of that list." He eyes the oversized beanbag in the corner, next to my bed, which I'm sure is still there under all my clothes—somewhere.

I smirk, shoving those same school papers into an already-crammed drawer. "I'm on it, Dad. Just have a ton of stuff going on; can't stop thinking about the cookie drive-through at Ralphs this week."

I pull my cropped JUILLIARD hoodie out of the hamper as Dad steps over a different pile of dirty clothes. He looks around for a place to sit, but everything is covered in layers of my stuff: scout stuff, cheerleading stuff, school stuff. I yank the hoodie over my head and button my white jeans with the tuxedo stripes down the sides. Dad is watching me closely as I walk over to my bed and heave a big ball of clean clothes onto the floor to make room for him. I step back and point. This only makes him rub his goatee and chuckle—but just a little.

"Hey, I'm trying." I shrug as Dad fake-grimaces.

"I'll help my Brookie with the room," Betty Jean says,

waltzing into my mess with her usual charm. She tucks her slouchy tee into her ripped jeans and winks at me.

"Thanks, Betty Jean," I say, fist-bumping her. "But is it okay if we do it later? The girls are on their way over so we can get all the last-minute stuff together for the cookie drive-through at Ralphs market."

"Ah, there's just nothing like cookie season," Dad says to Betty Jean. When he spies the angst in my eyes, he quickly adds, "It'll keep getting better, kiddo. And it sounds like a cookie drive-through is the exact thing needed to get your mojo back."

I stare into Mom's million-dollar smile in the picture on my dresser. "Did you guys know she used to say she was my silent partner?"

Dad's eyes linger on the photo, too. "She might've mentioned it to me a few times over the years."

"I had no idea how much she was silently doing behind the scenes." I get up from the bed and trudge over to my desk, but Betty Jean stops me for a snuggle.

"You might not know this," she whisper-shares into my hair, moving her single strand of pearls away from my forehead, "but I'm a bit of a business tycoon myself. Where do you think that pink Cadillac convertible in the driveway came from?"

"I'm sure there's a whole juicy story there, Betty Jean,"

I say as she kisses my forehead. "You're always good for one of those."

Before she can get into it, the doorbell rings.

It's the girls, I think, feeling lighter already.

I squeeze Betty Jean's hands to reassure her that I'm okay. Then I flash Dad a smile. "I'll get it!" I announce, dashing out of the room.

"Well, if you need me, I'll be right here. Like I always am!" Betty Jean says.

I peek out the window and spy Stella Rose, Lyric, and Lucy on the doorstep. I swing the door open, and they all yell in unison, "Cookie monster!"

Lyric takes a big gulp from her Starbucks cup and throws her other arm around me. "Today is a new day," she declares. "Ready to gobble up some cookie sales?"

I giggle when Lucy squeezes my cheek with her glittery blue-and-red nail tips, which match her tie-dyed blue-and-red romper. She made it herself. It's so adorable that a few girls at school have already preordered one from her shop. "It's your time, Sunshine," she says, blowing air-kisses around my face before beelining toward my room.

Stella Rose points her video camera at me, framing her shot just right. She adjusts her eyeglasses and motions for me to take a step closer. "You look divine in this natural light."

I stick out my tongue and bug my eyes, giggling into the lens. "Why are you filming me again?"

"Because the cookie race is on and popping." Stella Rose balks at me, as if I should understand her movie-making motives. "And I have to record every magical second of it for my doc." She follows me back to the room in her camo combat boots, narrating every step.

"Did I miss some big announcement about you shooting a documentary?"

Stella Rose puts her finger to her lips and shushes me. "It's a competition for kids about setting and reaching a big goal. I'm focusing on your magnificent cookie journey."

"That's dope, Stella Rose!" I say, high-fiving her.

"It's due in four weeks, but I'm struggling with the intro—you know, the part about me," she says, scrunching her face into a frown. "Ick! I hate being in front of the camera. I get all tongue-tied and nervous, and I can't get my words out."

"I can help you."

"Nope. Today it's all about helping you reclaim first place." She focuses the lens on my nose. "Now, just act natural for the camera."

"Okay," I say, obliging her with a smile before sticking

out my tongue. We both giggle, and then I shoo her and the camera lens away.

When I turn to see Dad greeting everyone, I cross my fingers, hoping he doesn't do anything cringeworthy.

"Good to see you again, girls," Dad says as he steps over multiple stacks of clothes scattered across the floor. I kick a few of the T-shirts and jeans into a corner and push him out the door. When I try to close it, his big foot gets in the way.

"Please don't embarrass me," I mutter at him, pressing my hands together for serious emphasis. "*Pretty* please."

"Perfect timing," Betty Jean sings from the hallway as she hustles toward the kitchen. "The brownies I put in the oven should almost be ready."

"She's *so* my shero!" Lucy proclaims, pulling both her iPad and her laptop from her bag.

"I promise to clean my room as soon as we're done," I plead with Dad, shoving my pinky in his face. "Swear." After a few seconds, he slowly inches his foot from the doorway. *Whew,* I think as I shut the door and turn to face the girls. Now we can get down to business.

"Well," Lucy starts, already beaming, "the supermarket confirmed our time this afternoon. We're all booked to set up our pop-up store in their parking lot."

I sit up straight and explain my mission. "Last year, I only sold fifty boxes, but I didn't have a whole pop-up store; it was just a table near the front door. So, this year, with all our bells and whistles, my goal is to sell a hundred! We preordered four hundred boxes. Now we just have to sell, sell, sell!"

Right on cue, Betty Jean opens the door and glides into the room with a tray of goodies in her hands. "I'd love to drive my cookie moguls to the supermarket and help set up your fab pop-up store. Someone will need to grab the inventory, of course, and we can't forget all the promo stuff." She hands off the tray, which is empty when it comes back to her.

Lucy closes her laptop. "Boom! Looks like we'll be all good in the cookie hood. Thanks, Betty Jean."

Betty Jean pops the imaginary collar on her white tee and blows a highlighted strand of hair from her eyes. "I happen to know a thing or two about sales, b-t-dubs."

"She means it, too. You know that pink drop-top Caddy in the driveway?"

"It's sick!" Lyric says, shaking her head. "I've always been smitten with that ride, Betty Jean."

"Funny story about how Bo Peep came into my life." Betty Jean nods, looking around for a place to sit. "Now, I don't want to take up time from your strategy sesh."

Lucy scoots over on the bed and smooths the top of my rumpled comforter. "But we want to hear all about it."

"It's a good one, too," she says, sitting down and crossing her legs. "I mean, it was a mighty tight race between me and Lola Lou, which surprised me because I didn't even see her coming. But in the end, that car had my name written all over it."

"What were you selling?" Stella Rose asks, resting her chin on her hand.

Betty Jean blushes and then makes a pretend mirror with the palm of her hand. She puckers her lips and exclaims, "Beauty!"

We all gasp and lean in closer.

"I'm what they call a Grand Achiever. I built a whole sales team and everything."

"How much lipstick did you have to sell to win that ride?" Lyric asks.

Betty Jean laughs. But then she gets really serious when she says, "Lots!"

"She's a total beauty girl," I explain to the room. "She's opening up her second beauty bar in LA. They're called Curls and Pearls." I hold up a handful of braids. "It's where the magic happens."

"You're something else, Betty Jean," Lyric says, swinging the chair from side to side. "Definitely my kinda girl."

Mine too, I think as I look up at my grandmother with pride. That's when the most dazzling idea pops into my head. "Hey, everyone," I call, trying to get their attention. "We might have stumbled upon our very own secret weapon." I turn to Betty Jean and press my hands together in prayer. "Betty Jean, you'd make a phenom Sunflower troop leader."

"O.M.Greatness! She totally would!" Lucy rages.

I press my hands together even harder. "We're kind of in need of one since Mom's not here anymore."

"That's a splendid idea," Stella Rose says, clapping her hands and chanting Betty Jean's name. "My sister would love to turn the reins over to you. She has no idea what she's doing." Then she shakes her head and shrugs. "None."

Betty Jean taps her chin and looks into each of our eager faces. "I've never been a troop leader before."

"You'd be purrr-fect," Lyric sings, tossing her venti Starbucks cup into the already-overflowing wastebasket. "Kind of like a mentor-mother mash-up."

"Sounds like an inspired way to spend—" But before she can finish, we all topple her with hugs. "My weekends."

"I know one thing," I say, coming up for air. "Piper Parker better watch out."

NINE

Betty Jean honks the horn one last time as we pull up to the stoplight across from the Ralphs supermarket on Olympic Boulevard Thursday after school. I watch her wave at all the people pointing at her and taking pictures of us in her infamous car. She loosens the knot on the pastel scarf that's been carefully tied under her chin so her hair doesn't get mussed. Today she's wearing a neat pony with sideswept bangs that really showcase her long neck and her signature single-strand pearls.

"Does this happen everywhere you go?" Lucy asks, her mouth gaping.

Betty Jean carefully parks the Cadillac in a spot near

the center entrance. "It's the car," she says, sliding her hand across the dashboard. "She's the eye candy."

Lyric adjusts the rhinestone headband that's decorating her topknot. "It's a total vibe, Betty Jean. And I'm here for it."

Betty Jean steps out of the car and pulls her classic white tee over her black leggings. She searches the crowd for the manager.

I cup my hand over my eyes. "He said he'd be waiting for us at the entrance."

"There he is," Betty Jean says, nodding at the lanky guy in the blue vest and brown pants who doesn't look a day over fifteen. He waves his hands around in the air, his caterpillar brows pinned, as he rushes over to our car. Betty Jean checks her watch and smiles approvingly. She insists that people keep their word about everything, especially when it comes to being on time. She always says that if you're on time, you're already late. Everywhere we go, we have to be fifteen minutes early—that's on time, according to her.

"Ms. Betty Jean Jones," he says, extending his hand. "I spoke with one of your girls on the phone." He oohs and aahs before reaching out to touch the Cadillac. Betty Jean smacks his hand away.

"Sorry, Ms. Betty Jean," he says, massaging his knuckles.

Wearing a wide grin, he fans himself. "Nice to finally meet the woman behind the wheels."

"You must be Jimmy," Betty Jean says, shaking his hand before shifting her attention to us—our cue to hop out of the car.

I step forward and smooth the wrinkles on my scout uniform before professionally introducing myself. "Hello, Jimmy. I'm Brooklyn Ace."

"Yes," Jimmy says. "Last year's big winner."

"Well, I didn't win it all, but that's the goal this year."

"Why don't we focus on making that happen? I set up everything just the way you asked," Jimmy says, pointing to the square behind us that's blocked off with orange cones. "This side of the parking lot is designated for you girls. The area inside the cones is all yours. I set up two tables for you as well. This way, it should be pretty easy for people to swing their cars around and grab their cookies."

"Thanks so much, Jimmy," I say, beaming. "This is pretty awesome. Our own cookie drive-through. Nice to see it finally come to life."

"That's some serious manifesting," Stella Rose says, bowing her head.

Lyric snaps her fingers. "It *is* pretty sweet!"

"Nobody's asked for this kind of setup before," Jimmy tells us.

Betty Jean folds her arms over her chest and says matter-of-factly, "My girls are thinking outside the box. They have big goals today."

"See, Jimmy, we want to maximize store space and minimize customer wait time," Lucy says over her shoulder as she pulls her faux-leather fingerless gloves over her hands and starts unloading cookies from the trunk.

"Our goal today is one hundred boxes." Lyric struggles to hoist a big box into the air. "Bottom line: We want to collect all the cheddar from your customers...after they're done shopping with you first, of course."

"Of course," I chime.

"Yes, of course," Jimmy agrees with a polite smile. "Well, I'll leave you girls to it, then. You've got three hours to rake it in before the next troop on the schedule tonight."

We hustle to finish setting up our shop in the rear of the parking lot. After about twenty minutes, we're ready with our monogrammed scout tablecloths, decorative posters, and cardboard signs with big black arrows. We take turns inspecting each other's scout uniforms, making sure the sashes and vests with our badges and pins are picture-perfect. Lucy steps back and gives each one of our red Converses a once-over.

"Pristine," she finally approves.

"Let's go!" I say, grabbing an iPad and pointing to the first cone. "I'll greet them when they drive up."

"Good job, girls," Betty Jean says, walking back from the car with a big World Scouts banner. She sets it on the ground next to the table, and I check my watch, wondering what's taking my backup dancers so long to get here. That's when I spy a few kids in Valentine Middle practice uniforms moving between a scooter and a blue sedan.

"They're here! They're here!" I yelp.

"You guys are late!" Lyric says to the kid with the tambourine. He turns to the boy with the clarinet and shrugs.

Lucy rolls her eyes. "Again, not my idea, but I guess you guys are unofficially part of the scout squad now!" She straightens the blue bow tie on the girl with the snare drum and then pats her on the shoulder.

"Thanks for coming," I say, looking around for Magic and the Stumbles, until I see Magic barreling out of her big sister's shiny SUV.

"Magic Olive Poindexter reporting for duty," Magic yells from a few parking spaces over. My heart finally settles when I see Winnie's tricked-out wheelchair and LuLu striding close behind her.

"Now that the gang's all here, we can get this party started!" I say, hugging my crew.

"We got you!" Winnie says, shaking her poms in the air.

The Stumbles and the band line up in front of the table with the huge cookie display. They check out the scene, eagerly awaiting their cue.

"It looks like we have our first customer," I say, jumping up and down as a maroon SUV pulls up to the first cone.

Lyric shoves her forefingers into her mouth to whistle until she gets the attention of the HoneyBees and the band. She points to Magic, who counts down the start of the HoneyBee signature dance routine.

"Five, six, five, six, seven, eight," Magic snaps her fingers as the cymbals bang together and the drum beats erratically.

It's go time, I think as I take a closer look at the driver and recognize the sweet lady with the twin boys in the back seat. She used to work in the main office at Valentine Middle when she became one of my first regulars.

"Hi, Ms. Bailey. It's so good to see you."

"Brooklyn! I was wondering if I'd see you again this year selling those delicious cookies I love so much. It's my favorite thing about the new year, and you are my cookie girl, after all." She reaches into her purse for her wallet. "I like the new setup. Now I can keep the cookies stashed in the car while I run into the store and grab a few things. Pretty smart, girls." She waves her wallet out the window. "I bet this'll be how you win again."

I turn to all the different boxes of cookies stacked in cool pyramids on the table and cross my fingers. "Here's hoping, Ms. Bailey. I'm shooting for the Santa Monica title this year."

"Well then, let me get my order in promptly. I think I'll have four boxes of the Chocolate Marvels and four boxes of the Peanut Butter Babies." She gives it some thought and then adds, "You know what? Why don't we splurge and go with four boxes of the Shortbread Shorties, too?"

"Whoa, that's a pretty big order, Ms. Bailey. You usually stick to your two faves."

"You remember that?" she asks, surprised. "You have tons of customers and you remember my little order?"

"Of course I do; you're very important to me."

She reaches for my hand and squeezes it like my mom used to do whenever I needed a little extra encouragement. "You will always have my support, Brooklyn. I'm so proud of you for continuing this, even with your mom gone. She would be really proud of you."

"Thank you, Ms. Bailey." I beam at the woman, who has always been so supportive. And I know she's right: Mom would be thrilled about our pop-up shop. *Maybe today will be the day I turn it all around*, I think as I type Ms. Bailey's order into the form on the tablet screen. Before I can send it to Stella Rose to fulfill, another customer pulls behind Ms. Bailey. I wave to let them know they're next. When I look up from the screen, another car pulls up—and then another.

"Okay, Ms. Bailey. Well, um..." I know I'm feeling flustered when I start fidgeting with the gold rings wrapped around my braids. I tug too hard on one and it pops off. "Um, you can pull forward and pay Lyric. Lucy will have your cookies waiting for you."

I wave goodbye as she pulls up to the next cone to pay Lyric.

There isn't enough time to celebrate the first order as I turn to greet the next customer, grumpy Old Man Struthers. He orders his usual, Coconut Cravings and Shorties, and I send him on his way, ignoring his lopsided toupee.

"Look at all the action we're getting," Lyric says, standing on her tiptoes to check out the long line that's formed. She wraps a flyaway tendril around her topknot and poses for Stella Rose, who picks up her camera and snaps a few shots. "This is beyond fab!"

"Yeah," I say, anxiously waving the next car forward.

Lyric nods at the band, and the girl with the drums starts a new, even louder beat. Magic twirls around the table and LuLu kicks her leg into the air while Winnie waves her pom-poms around her head.

Stella Rose watches the frenzied scene, wipes her forehead, and huffs. "We're just getting started and I'm tired already."

Betty Jean giggles from the lawn chair she set up behind the table, next to the cashbox. "Stella Rose, your shift just started. You're not even an hour into it."

"I didn't think we'd have a traffic jam," she admits when the cars in the back of the line start to honk their horns.

I adjust my sash and rub my palms together. "I need to move faster. The line is wrapping around the parking lot, and some of the cars are starting to block spots. We definitely don't want to spark any road rage today."

Before I can race through the next order, I get distracted when I hear very familiar music blasting in the distance. As it gets closer, I realize it's the infamous ice cream truck tune. I look up, down, and around the parking aisles. Then I spot it—right behind the blue Santa Monica bus. An actual World Scouts cookie truck! And Piper Parker is hanging out its window, wearing a tiara, waving at everyone as it passes.

"Scout cookies! Scout cookies!" Piper yells into her bullhorn. "Come get your yummy World Scouts cookies!"

Stella Rose gasps over the music as the decked-out truck pulls into the other side of the parking lot. "Do you guys see that? She has a food truck! A COOKIE FOOD TRUCK!"

This time, Lyric and Stella Rose wave their arms around, signaling the band to jump-start another, less drab song.

"Five, six, and five, six, seven, eight," Magic yells, counting down the beginning of a routine as LuLu and Winnie shake their poms with more oomph than before. Fighting for the crowd's attention is taking everything out of them—and me.

"From the east, to the west!" Magic yells out behind me. "Brooklyn's cookies are the best!"

Lyric isn't feeling very rah-rah as she crosses her arms over her chest when more prospective customers make the hike to the cookie truck. We all watch Piper wave her hand around in the air like a pageant queen before adjusting her tiara.

"Oh no she didn't!" Lyric grimaces. "Who does she think she is?"

Lucy passes Mr. Struthers his cookies and throws her fist in the air. "This is our turf."

"We'll get everyone's attention, B," Magic tries to reassure me.

"We know just what to do," says Lu.

Winnie takes a deep breath. "We have a few secret weapons of our own."

Magic swipes at the sweat dripping down her fore-head while Winnie shakes out her arms before massaging them. Magic yells, "Okay, Winn, do your thing!" as the band girl with the snare drum pounds down on it furiously.

"Gimme a B!" Magic shouts while Winnie pops a wheelie in her chair. "Gimme an R!" Magic hits a slightly awkward toe touch. When she lands, Winnie rolls back and forth on her wheels until she finally spins around, stopping right in front of Stella Rose, who gasps and drops an armful of cookies onto the pavement. A loud screech from the clarinet causes us all to smush our palms over our ears.

"Make it stop!" Lucy stomps her feet and waves her hands for the band to halt the music. She rushes behind a group of teenagers with skateboards who look back and forth between Piper and me. "We're selling cookies, too, guys!" A few seconds pass before they shrug and skate toward my sales nemesis.

A lady with a cane chuckles as she gets into her car. "A real-life cookie face-off."

Two of the cars at the end of our line head over to the ultracool food truck that's been professionally wrapped with pictures of all the cookies around it. One by one, our customers hop out of their cars and rush to greet Piper, who eats it all up, waving and grinning triumphantly in our direction. I shrug, pretending to be unbothered, until a few more people park their cars and walk over to her truck, too. I turn to my scout squad and fume, confused. "What are we supposed to do?"

Lyric gasps. "She's literally stealing our customers! Again!"

I furrow my brows and pout, asking Betty Jean, "Can she even do that?"

"She's good," Betty Jean says, standing up. She slips her hands into her pockets. "The girl's got drive, that's for sure. She's technically not infringing on your designated area; she's not even taking up any of your space. She pulled the truck into a single parking spot and that's allowed. It's actually pretty genius." Betty Jean nods and sucks her teeth. "So yeah, she can do that."

"But Piper's committing cookie-customer theft!" I declare as three more people decide to give her their business.

The StumbleBees, ignoring the mayhem in the parking lot, remain focused. Winnie wheels herself to the left side to sit as anchor. She nods at each of them, shaking her pom-poms around her head and giving a good Honey-Bee face. On cue, the Stumbles lock eyes and rush to link arms for a kick line. LuLu's foot shoots behind her head while Magic's monogrammed HoneyBee sneakers barely hit hip level. But she yells out anyway, calling for the next letter in my name. "Gimme an O!" The disjointed band yells back, "O!"

"Just…no!" Lucy gripes. Furiously, she shakes her head as the kick line starts to move backward, straight toward the table display. Magic tries with all her might to kick her leg higher, but her body has other plans. At first, it's just a little wobble from side to side, but then the uncontrollable head bobbling *with* the torso floundering happens.

"Don't! Magic, stop!" I yell in her direction, trying to warn her, but she loses her balance and falls headfirst into the stacked pyramid of cookies. And just like that, it all comes tumbling down.

TEN

I glance out the window for the fifteenth time since the clock struck six. Now it's too dark to see past the end of the block, but every time a car turns onto our street, the curtains light up and I race back to the window. I watch the little red sports car blaze by our house and turn the corner.

Sigh.

The clock now shows 8:02 PM.

I march into the kitchen and grab the Doritos before heading into the living room to set them on the coffee table beside the Flamin' Hot Cheetos. After the day I've had, it's definitely time for Netflix and Chips with my girls. I need it now more than ever. I mean, I've been feeling a mix of overwhelming dread and, frankly, devastation after the disastrous cookie drive-through.

Okay, so here are the deets: Our drive-through sales weren't what we wanted them to be, to say the least. Word was that after Piper left the Ralphs supermarket, she hit up the Pier, then rolled down Main Street to hang outside Urth Caffé before completing her rounds in Venice at the world-famous Muscle Beach. Our cookie pop-up, on the other hand, ended up causing a massive traffic jam, and store customers couldn't get in or out of their parking spots. And to pile on, I've been quietly journaling about what Dr. Simone called grief. Such a little word that causes some seriously big feelings.

But none of that matters tonight, I think, as the curtains light up and I speed-walk back to the window to check again and...Bingo!

I swing the front door open to greet my scout squad.

"Cookie monster!" they yell as they bolt past me in matching jogger suits, blowing smooches into the air like the really rich and sophisticated.

"You're late!" I yell back, grabbing the oversized bowl of popcorn from Betty Jean. She air-kisses the girls before ducking back into the kitchen. I smirk at my squad and fuss, "You were just supposed to go home and change into your comfies. What took you so long?"

"OMG!" Stella Rose starts. "Arlo had to pick Ollie up from soccer practice, and I had to wait for him to get back to give me a ride, but then—"

"Your brother Arlo"—Lyric's eyes twinkle as she shoves one hand into the bowl of Doritos and her other hand into the Hot Cheetos—"is so ca-yoot!"

"*Nawt!*" Stella Rose screeches into the air, grabbing the popcorn from me and plopping down on the couch between Lyric and Lucy. "Then Sarabeth started vomiting because of her period, and I had to—"

"Now, that's an *ew* from me!" Lucy spouts, pretending to gag on the popcorn that she just shoved into her mouth.

"Which part?" Stella Rose asks Lucy, throwing her hands in the air. "We're young women. We're all going to get our periods."

"I'm not," Lucy says smugly, before shuddering at the thought. "Period."

I lock eyes with Lyric, and we both giggle at the funny Lucy doesn't even realize she's made. Then I think about it and add, "I haven't yet. But I'm twelve, sooo I'm sure Aunt Flo is coming to visit soon."

"Your aunt is coming over to Netflix and Chips with us?" Stella Rose asks, looking around.

"Girl." Lyric tugs on Stella Rose's pink joggers. "It's just something us women say."

Stella Rose shakes her head, and I take pity on her and hop into an explanation. "My mom used to call her period Aunt Flo." Stella Rose's eyebrows dig deeper into her head. "Because your period has a flow. You know, light, medium, heavy. It's on all the tampon boxes."

"Gawwwd!" Lucy yells, falling into the couch cushion, pretending to be dead. "Can we puh-lease change the subject!"

"My mom always says that she's checking into the Red Roof Inn for the week," Lyric announces, laughing. We all look at each other and burst out laughing, too.

"Soooo, young women," Lucy says, standing over us. "Which epi of *The Baby-Sitters Club* are we watching?" We stop laughing when she shoves her hands into her hips, clearly done with this convo.

"I haven't seen any of them," Stella Rose admits, hiding her face behind a cushion.

"Okay, no probs," I say, watching Lucy's face transform into a snarl, being the perfect antonym for *patience*.

I grab the remote and point it toward the television, ignoring Lucy's dramatics. "It's no biggie; we'll start from the beginning."

We snuggle together and settle in, and we all follow rule number one: Nobody gets to say a word during *BSC*.

We watch one episode after another until Lucy's stomach growls.

"Pizza's here, girls!" Dad calls out from the front door, almost as soon as the third episode ends.

"Perfect timing, Mr. Ace," Lucy peps, gripping her belly, "because my stomach is starting to eat itself."

Dad walks into the room and places three pizza boxes on the wooden coffee table. Betty Jean pads into the room behind him and sets out plastic utensils, paper plates, and cups. She looks around at the extra blankets and the pillows that are still scattered around "just in case anyone dozes off," she'd said earlier, before the gang arrived.

Betty Jean takes the pitcher of lemonade from Dad. "Now. You girls should be all set." She places it in front of the pizza boxes and smacks her lips together. "Looks like a perfect marathon night made especially for my cookie moguls."

We dig into the pepperoni, the sausage, and the veggie pizzas, leaving only a few slices in each cardboard box. I reach for a sausage, but when the doorbell rings, I rush to answer it instead. I already know who it is, so when I open the door and see my fave Stumble on the other side, I throw my arms around Magic and utter, "You're late!"

"Sorry," Magic says, hugging me back. "But I brought

you something." She digs into her Wonder Woman bag and pulls out five packs of Twizzlers. "One for each of us," she says as I close the door behind her.

We fist-bump into one big explosion, then head back into the living room, where the girls are deep in analysis mode.

"No, I think I'm more like Stacey," Lyric pipes up, shoving her sun-kissed tendrils behind her ear. "She's from New York and she's sophisticated. So...obvi."

"And she likes alllll the boys," Lucy says, giggling and pointing at Lyric.

"Who's Stacey?" Stella Rose asks, looking around the room for answers.

"She's introduced in the first epi," Lucy huffs. She taps her chin, then says, "I'm definitely Kristy."

"I think Mary Anne and me would be friends in real life," Magic says, cozying into the couch.

I fall back onto the cushions beside her and grip the closest blanket. "She could def give me some pointers— like how to survive this life thing without Mom."

"Did you pick up any grief tools in therapy?" Lyric asks, grabbing more Hot Cheetos.

I shrug. "She gave me a journal."

Lucy shoves a bunch of Doritos into her mouth and says, "The only thing my babysitter's therapist gave her was the flu once."

Magic rests her hand on my shoulder. "Have you written in the journal?"

"Today," I answer. "After the disaster at the market." I grip the blanket tighter. "Dr. Simone thinks it's a good idea to write down some of my scary thoughts."

Lucy shakes her head and rubs her belly. "I went home and downed a pint of Chunky Monkey."

We sit quietly, each with our own memories of the pitiful pop-up shop. Then I finally break the silence and say, "I worked out some and showered. I tried really hard not to drive myself bananas over tomorrow's Week Two cookie tally at school. Can't say I was successful." I sulk deeper into the sofa. "Then I scribbled some stuff down."

"You wanna read some of it to us?" Stella Rose asks, but not really asking.

Lucy points to my bedroom. "Go get your journal, B."

"You guys don't want to hear that stuff," I say, waving them off.

Lyric motions for me to skedaddle to my room. "Uh, of course we do! You wrote it, didn't you?"

A few seconds later, I'm back in the room with my crew, my journal in my hand as I find my spot on the couch. I stare at the notebook nervously.

"You're really brave," Magic says, biting into a Twizzler

and shaking it at me. "Dealing with all the stuff about your mom...it's inspiring."

I hadn't thought of it that way. "Some days I feel like I'm barely hanging on."

Magic rests her head on my shoulder, and I sigh.

"Read to us what you've got," Stella Rose says, pulling a blanket over her knees. "We're all ears."

"Okay, well," I start, "it's mostly, like, just random thoughts that I shaped into a sloppy poem, mainly because I didn't have to turn it into Mr. Reynolds or anything."

"Doesn't matter. They're your thoughts and we're here for it," Lyric says, moving closer to Stella Rose and stealing some of the blanket.

"Okay, here goes," I say, and clear my throat.

I turn to the second page of the journal and stare at the words. The corners of the pages are crinkled and some of the ink is splotchy from my tears that refused to stop falling. I read the first word to myself: *MOM*.

Then I wait. And luckily, no one pushes.

"'Mom,'" I start, out loud this time.

I squirm around on my butt. Then I tread slowly through my written thoughts.

I see you
I call you

I remember loving you.
Mom.
Yellow
Sunshine
Red
Blue
I still feel all the colors of you.
Mom.
Beats
Lyrics
Hymns
Melodies
You singing in bed with me.
Mom.
Crying to sleep
I can barely see
Is God even listening
Please...come back to me.
Mom.

I look up from reading and exhale. Then I muddle through the last few words, holding back tears, to finish.

I promise I'll be good.

Stella Rose sniffles. And when Lyric sniffles behind her, she catches herself and coughs, waving it off. "Dope." And that's all she says while she snaps her fingers and bows her head.

"It's just a few words I jotted down. My chest felt heavy thinking about not seeing my name on the cookie tally board tomorrow. And Dr. Simone said when that happens, I should get it on the page."

"B, you're a total Claudia," Magic says, grinning. "A true artist."

"At this point," I start, admitting the truth to my girls, "I really think I'll try anything to make the gnawing pain less, well, painful."

"Did that help?" Magic asks, nodding at the wet page.

"Maybe...I guess...well," I stammer. "I mean...I'm not sure." I pull my knees to my chest and think about it. "It's just that no matter what I do, the feeling of doom doesn't ever really go away. It feels like it just kind of wiggles around in my body, and when it crawls up to my brain, I'm forced to think about how much it hurts. And that's when—" I realize I'm rambling, so I stop.

Stella Rose grips her neck and leans closer. "When what?"

"Well, that's when the walls start to move closer to

me, and my head feels all clogged up with heaviness. It's like blurry white fuzz."

"Intense." Lucy pulls her legs up to her chest, too.

"Yeah," I mutter. "Tell me about it."

Lyric reaches over Stella Rose and takes the journal from my grip. She holds out her hand until Lucy digs into her bag and gives her a red pen. Not wasting any time, she jots something onto one of the pages. Then she hands it back to me and I read it aloud, "'I need help with the pain. Please do your job.'"

Lucy giggles as Stella Rose whisper-sighs, "You're juggling a lot for a twelve-year-old."

"See, B. It's like I said." Magic scoots close enough to me to cup her hands over her mouth and whisper, "Brave."

A few episodes of *BSC* later, Betty Jean barrels out of the kitchen with a tray of cupcakes.

"Cupcakes can only mean one thing," Lyric sings.

"No, uh-uh," Stella Rose exhales, reaching for a cupcake and rejecting Lyric's line of thinking.

Lyric balls up a napkin and tosses it at me. "It's truth-or-dare time!"

Her excitement is contagious, I have to admit; I feel it lift me from my gray haze.

"This'll get you vibrating at a higher frequency," Stella

Rose says to me, biting into a red velvet cupcake. "That's what today's affirmation was all about."

"Cupcakes?" Lucy asks, smirking.

"No, silly." Stella Rose takes out her phone and scrolls around until she finds what she's looking for. She rests her palm over my knee. "'I manifest love, prosperity, happiness, and an abundance of all good things.'"

"I'm first for truth or dare," Lucy declares, ignoring Stella Rose and taking a huge bite out of the chocolate cupcake. But it's like she can't make up her mind and reaches for a vanilla one and chomps into that one, too.

I mouth *Thank you* to Stella Rose before turning to Lucy. "Okay, Luce, truth or—"

"Dare!" she yells, bouncing up and down on the couch, not needing to think about it.

"Hmm," Lyric starts. "I dare you to—"

"Wait!" Lucy stands up, shaking her head. She swallows... hard. "I changed my mind. Give me truth. Yeah, I want truth."

"Ooo-kay," Lyric says, making a steeple with her fingers. She lifts her right eyebrow into her forehead and chuckles. "What, exactly, is your grade in math?"

"No!" She sits back down. "I want dare. I changed my mind again."

"You can't change twice," Stella Rose clarifies. "Those are the rules."

"Still your turn, Luce," I say, not letting her off the hook.

When I shift my attention back to Lucy, she's stalling—oldest trick in the book. I clock her time and she waits sixty more seconds before professing her truth. I know because I'm staring at the clock at the bottom of the screen saver on the TV that keeps flashing pretty pictures of mountains and lakes and icebergs.

"Fine, a D...minus," she mumbles, startling me. I thought she was going to find some way to back out of fessing up.

"A what?" Magic asks, leaning forward, unable to hear her from this end of the couch.

Lucy crosses her arms over her chest and barks, "My grade is a D minus, okay?!"

Stella Rose covers her mouth with her palm. "Whoa! What'd your mom say?"

Lucy shrugs and whisper-explains, "I didn't tell her." And before anyone can challenge her, she spouts, "I know she'd put me on strict punishment, and I wouldn't be able to run my store." She props her elbows on her knees and rests her head in her hands. "And I have a big shipment of materials coming for the new spring line of accessories in a few days." She glares at Lyric. "I don't see you being open with your mom." Lucy smirks, crossing her arms over her chest, as she challenges Lyric. "Your turn next. Truth or dare?"

"Dare," Lyric says, getting tangled in a stare-down with Lucy. "Let's just get it over with."

"Okay," Lucy starts, looking around the room at each of us. "I dare you to call your mom and tell her that you need her help with your big audition for the school musical."

Magic leans over and mutters into my ear, "What's the big deal about that?"

"She really doesn't like to ask for help," I explain. "And that's just the beginning."

Magic scrunches her face into a bunch of wrinkles. "But why not? It's her mom."

Stella Rose leans over my lap and checks in with Magic. "Have you met Lyric?"

I tap Magic on the knee. "She's just not...the most vulnerable one in the group."

Stella Rose grabs a peanut butter cupcake from the tray and bites into it, declaring, "And rejection hurts."

"Especially from your mom," I whisper to Magic as Lyric takes out her phone and stares at it.

"But why wouldn't her mom help her with her—"

I grab Magic's hand and squeeze it until she stops talking.

Lyric scrolls through her phone. "Seriously, Lucy?"

Lucy nods.

Lyric stops on a picture of her mom. "This feels personal."

"Consider it a push," Lucy clarifies, smizing with her eyes.

"Off a cliff," Lyric quips, finally calling her mother.

We all sit in silence, each of our eyes saucering in the intense moment.

Lyric scoots to the edge of the couch, biting on her nails as the phone rings and rings... and rings. But then... voice mail!

"Leave a message," Lucy orders. "Don't hang up, that's the dare."

Lyric rolls her eyes and begins. "Hi, Mom. It's me. I, uh, need your—" Lyric shoves her free hand under her butt and winces. "I, uh, have a big audition and I was wondering if you could *help* me with song selection. And maybe with the song, too. I know you're super busy with—" Then she just stops talking. And then the message cuts off. "There. I asked her."

I clap for her efforts. Magic joins me in applause and starts to whistle.

"You took the first step," I say to Lyric. "Now I'm sure she'll be happy to help you."

Lyric smiles and starts to exhale just as she gets a text. Lucy hovers over her shoulder.

"It's her mom," Lucy says, eyeing Lyric's phone.

Lyric hides the phone and reads the text. She takes her time before turning back to us. "She says she's really busy. But...she said I should ask my aunt Jackie. And"— she reads from the screen—"'next time for sure, Boogie. You got this! Go knock 'em dead.'"

I hop up from the couch when I spy more than a few tears in my friend's eyes. And she never cries. Like never. As in ever.

I settle in next to her and rock her back and forth when she covers her face and slowly starts to sob. None of us saw this coming.

Stella Rose glares at Lucy, who looks away.

"I didn't mean to make her cry," Lucy says. "It was just a dumb dare."

Lyric shakes her head and sighs. She wipes her tears away with the back of her palm. I've never seen her with her walls down before. She looks at the snowcapped Alps on the TV screen and says, "Sometimes, maybe...I wish she would make time for me, too."

"She still loves you," Lucy says, raising her shoulders up to her earlobes.

"Duh!" Lyric scoffs. "I *know* she loves me."

"I'll totally help you pick a song," Magic says from across the couch. "I'm not the singing type, but I know good music. I mean, have you heard Girl Power?!" Magic breaks out in song, wailing her fave vintage chart-topper, "Monster."

We all giggle at Magic's rendition of the popular song.

"I'll help you pick a song, too," I offer, even though I know this goes way deeper than a song. "We can all pick one together. I was thinking about Beyoncé or maybe even that lady from England with the really big voice." I look around the room at my crew for help. "You know, the one who always sings those really sad songs after her break-ups, making you wanna scarf down tubs of ice cream."

"Oh. You mean"—Stella Rose snaps her fingers—"Adele."

"Yeah, her." I turn back to Lyric. "You'd crush one of her songs."

"I'm fine," Lyric says, pulling away from me, from us all. "I shouldn't have bothered her in the first place. I know how important touring is." She wipes her face and straightens. "She's probably doing sound check or something. I'll just sing a vintage Beyoncé bop."

"I bet your mom thinks you've got it all handled," Stella Rose answers. "You usually do."

Lucy tries to get back in our good graces. "Your grades are top-notch. And you stay on schedule and you—"

"But she needs her mom," I say, completely understanding.

And as I sit in my living room with the leftovers of my mom's magical life all around us, I get it. I sink into the sofa and think about tomorrow's big cookie tally day and sigh. Boy, do I get it.

More than I wish I did.

ELEVEN

Fridays have become my new least favorite day of the week. There's something about the looming disappointment that just sits there, thick in the air. *I hate it*, I think as I trudge down the hall toward the cookie tally board outside Principal Pootie's office with Lyric next to me, skipping to a beat in her head. I'm basically walking in slow motion.

"Really, why are you speed-walking?" I ask. "What's the rush to get to the disappointment, espesh after everyone around Montana Ave ignored me and then, dare I mention, the abysmal cookie drive-through!"

She pulls me along—seemingly ignoring my whining—straight down the hallway packed with kids eager to leave. Count me in with that group, only I have to do this one huge thing first: Check the dumb cookie tally!

I fight through the tense pout that's smeared across my face when kids wave at me as I plod past their lockers. I nod and toss back a series of waves to kids I recognize.

"I have a surprise for you," Lyric says.

"Your mom's endorsement?" I ask, trying to sound low-pressure.

"Well…I wasn't going to say anything, but I did a thing."

"What kind of thing?" I ask, my eyebrows dipping deeper into my face.

"You'll be happy to know that I called her—again—and left three voice messages."

"You did that for me?" I screech. "Even after she told you she couldn't help you with your song?"

"Indeed." Lyric tosses her arm over my shoulder. "For clarification, she didn't say she wouldn't help *you*."

"True. True."

"Now I'm just waiting for her to call me back. I think she's in Baltimore. Or wait, maybe she's in Boston. Or maybe it was Buffalo."

"I hope she comes through for us. I really need a miracle."

"No matter what happens, we still have two more weeks," Stella Rose says, looping her arm through mine when we meet up with her and Lucy in front of the bulletin board.

"And anything can happen in two weeks," Lucy says, leaning into us.

Stella Rose positions her camera in front of my face. "You ready for the big reveal?"

I glance at the bulletin board:

VALENTINE MIDDLE
WORLD SCOUTS COOKIE SALES
WEEK 2 RANKINGS

I cover my eyes and shuffle my feet. "I can't look. I can't look."

"Well, seems like you have ants in your pants," Lyric says. "So I won't make you wait."

"In fifth place," Lucy starts.

"Is Ivory Sandberg," Stella Rose says in my left ear.

"Aaand... Rita Argyle is in fourth," Lucy says into my right one.

"What?" I yelp, completely stumped. "Oh no! Maybe this means that I didn't place at all this week." I make the sign of the cross and wait for my squad to tell me the bad news.

"And the third place goes to..."

"To Brooklyn Ace," Principal Pootie says from somewhere over me. "Good job, Ms. Ace." I peek through my fingers covering my eyes and see him staring at the cookie tally, dabbing his kerchief around his shiny forehead. "And second place belongs to Margaret Miller, with Piper Parker taking the top spot," Pootie adds, rocking back and forth on his scuffed loafers.

The school photographer rushes up to me and snaps a few shots.

"How's it feel?" he asks, shoving a pint-sized microphone in my face.

"How's what feel, exactly?" Lucy snarls at him. "Why don't you tell us how it feels to be an instigator?"

"Aw, c'mon, Brooklyn. Why don't you give me a sound bite I can use for the paper? Just tell me how it feels to come in third behind the new girl, especially after you prematurely declared yourself the big winner!"

I do my best to hide my disappointment, and boy am I relieved when Pootie takes the camera from him, leading him away by his collar. "Here at Valentine Middle, son, we have to always display good sporting spirit. It's part of our mission."

"Well," I say over my shoulder as I head toward the gymnasium for cheer practice, "I think I'm going to need a miracle."

Later that afternoon, cheer practice seems to drag on forever. I'm already feeling like a cookie loser, and to make matters worse, the HoneyBees are prepping for a big district competition in three weeks, and our routine is the antonym of *championship*. So, you see, not to be a drama queen, but this feeling of defeat is taking over my little life.

When we run through the routine again, my turns are subpar, and my feet feel like boulders smashing against the hardwood. I grapevine through the second eight-counts, barely able to hear the beat of the music, and kick my leg into the air. It's supposed to be a high kick, but it looks like my foot is dangling from my leg in need of medical attention. This can't be good, I think, when I'm supposed to transition into a new formation and lead the squad through the next chunk of the choreography. But I get confused and can't remember which side of the court is the front, so I end up in the back of the triangle instead of at the point.

"Stop! Stop!" Coach yells, her frizzy bangs bouncing above her eyes. "Brooklyn, you're clunking, not gliding, through most of the routine." Coach Cassidy is even more annoyed with me than when she told me the same thing five minutes ago. She walks onto the court and stands on top of the big honeybee's wings. She bends down and says, "Remember to focus, and, honey, you have to use your technique; think of yourself as limber and agile."

"Coach, I'm not feeling so agile right now. More like fragile."

"Let's take five and then run through the routine again." Coach turns to the team and says, "Everyone, rest for a few and grab some water."

"I don't need water, I need mojo," I sulk into the hot air.

"You'll get it," Magic says as we head off the court toward the bleachers. "It took me the whole first semester to learn the step routine."

"Yeah, and it took me even longer to be able to stand on Cappie's shoulders and not want to faint from feeling dizzy," LuLu says, joining our pity party.

"Thanks, guys," I say as Winnie rolls over to us. She readjusts her high pony and leans closer to me. "What's got you so scattered today?"

"Did you see the cookie rankings?" I roll my eyes and sigh.

"Nope. I refuse to look at anything that'll take me out of my zen zone," she declares.

"Is there anything we can do?" Magic asks. "You know, to help some more with sales or with—"

"Piper Parker!" Winnie barks. "After that stunt she pulled at the supermarket, I'm here for the revenge."

"I need some of that energy," I fess up. "I've been feeling kind of defeated lately, for obvi reasons."

"I get it," LuLu says.

"Same," Magic agrees. "You know, we're here to help you get through some of that if you need us."

I look at the Stumbles, and I don't want them feeling sorry for me. I decide to tell them about some of the stuff I've been using as my mental medicine. "I went back to see Dr. Simone. And it was cool. She even gave me a journal that's helping me sort through all my mom stuff. I'm starting to realize that everything is connected."

LuLu gulps down her water, then she looks at me and says, "Preach, sister."

Magic squeezes my shoulder. "It's not always easy to keep hard appointments. Just know that I'm proud of you."

"What kind of stuff are you writing about?" LuLu asks, scooting closer. "Lately, I've been writing, too, but it's mostly about my parents and their divorce."

"That's cool, Lu," Magic says. "Does that help you?"

LuLu shrugs. "It mostly makes me feel sad, but it's for

that assignment Mr. Reynolds gave us, the one about our autobiographies." LuLu gets down on the floor and eases into a stretch. "It's my truth, so if he wants to read all that dark stuff, then it's his funeral."

"I didn't know you were doing that," I say.

"And we didn't know you were in therapy. See, sharing is caring," Winnie says, sitting up straight and squaring her shoulders. "For his assignment, I'm writing about being the first girl with a disability on the HoneyBees."

"Sweet!" Magic says. "A real trailblazer, like my Grammy Mae." Magic gets on the floor next to LuLu and helps her with her stretch. She pulls Lu's leg behind her head and presses for a few seconds before easing up. "What are you writing about in therapy, B?"

"Mostly the dark stuff, kind of like Lu. The prompt I'm working on now is why it's hard to let go of the pain. That one's a doozy. And I def don't have an answer for it."

"I guess the emotions from divorce and death can be connected," Magic says, looking back and forth between me and Lu.

"Grief and sadness are like first cousins," I offer. "The ones that spend all the holidays together."

"Well, I'm here for both of you, whatever you need, and I'm always down to bring the snacks." Magic checks her watch, then says, "And today I'll be your therapy buddy again—if you want."

I look at the Stumbles, knowing that we just want each other to be happy.

"Girls! Let's hit the floor for the routine," Coach says, turning on the hip-hop song and blasting it through the gymnasium.

I grin back at Magic when she grabs my hand and pulls me up from the bleachers. She was a really good therapy buddy last time.

The bass bounces off the walls and envelops us all. Coach motions for our attention. "Get in formation; we have work to do to win this competition."

"Yeah, B, let's get in formation so we can set ourselves up for the big win," Magic says, referring to something much bigger than cheerleading. "I'll meet you at your locker after practice, and we can walk over together."

Cheer practice is turning out to be the exact mojo I needed. I head to my spot in formation, realizing that the big race isn't over.

"Hey, Magic," I say, feeling inspired. "I'd really like that."

TWELVE

After practice, I decided to keep my promise to my girls—and to myself. And if I'm being honest, it couldn't have come at a better time.

Therapy with Dr. Simone: Round Three.

"So," Magic asks as we sit in the waiting area of my stylish therapist's office. "What color bow tie do you think she's going to be wearing today?"

"Hmm, good question."

"I bet it's blue."

"I'm thinking maybe gold or yellow in honor of the Golden State."

Dr. Simone opens her door and waves at us. "You can come in now, Brooklyn."

Magic waves back at her before turning to me to say, "Purple with stripes."

"Didn't see that coming," I giggle, nodding at Dr. Simone.

Before I can walk away, Magic tugs on the patchy sleeve of my denim jacket. "I'm hashtag proud. You got this," she says, before snapping her fingers into an imaginary heart. "And I'll be right here, waiting for you."

"Froyo on you?" I ask.

"Of course," she says, winking at me. "And I invited the other girls, too, for an extra pick-me-up."

"Aw, Magic. Très cool."

"Well," she says, doing the funky chicken dance in her seat. "You know how we like to party."

"You ready, Brooklyn?" Dr. Simone asks, stepping back into her office.

"Coming," I say, and grab my journal from the end table, already daydreaming about mango froyo.

As Dr. Simone closes the door, I take my same seat in the room. The velvety sofa cushions don't feel as hard as they did earlier in the week when I was here. I guess my butt is adjusting.

"So, Brooklyn, how have you been since I saw you last?"

"Well, uh…I, uh, I…" I stammer, looking around at those same taupe curtains. "I guess I've been doing… fine."

Dr. Simone crosses her legs, and the bottom of her jeans rises above her ankle to reveal rainbow-striped socks with the word *HAPPY* stitched into them.

"Cool socks, Doc," I marvel.

"Cool sneaks," she says, checking out my custom rainbow-checkered Vans.

If we were anywhere but here, I'd probably really like Dr. Simone, but there's just something about being in this room with all my jumbled feelings that makes it kind of hard to look at her as a friend.

"I see Magic decided to come with you again," she says, glancing at the door.

"Yeah, she refuses to let me come without her." I grin. "Plus she promised me Pinkberry with my scout squad when we're done."

"Sounds like my kind of friend."

I think of Magic and can only say, "You know when you asked me how I'd describe her? Well, I was thinking, and she's like the sweetest frosting on top of your favorite birthday cake."

"Whoa, that's pretty sweet."

"And she never judges me." I scoot back into the sofa and start to relax. "She says I'm brave because I'm trying to deal with my mom, you know, not being here anymore. And not running from it." Then I think for a second and decide to be completely transparent. "Although I did want to run to Pinkberry today instead of coming to see you." Then I backpedal. "No offense."

"None taken," she says, laughing. "Gotta love Pinkberry."

"I know, huh," I agree, wiping my forehead and exhaling, relieved to have gotten that off my chest.

"Why don't you tell me how you've been feeling the last few days?"

"Well." I pick at the cuticle on my left pinky. "It's been kind of like a roller coaster. Sometimes I'm doing just fine coasting through the day, handling all my stuff at school or at home, at practice, or with my scout squad. But then, other times, I'll smell something, and it reminds me of my mom. Or other times, I'll see something, and it reminds me of mom. Or... then I mostly feel small. It's like I'm not strong enough to deal with all this stuff."

"What about those feelings makes you feel small?"

"Because it still hurts. And no matter what I do, I can't seem to make it feel any better, you know, on the inside."

I open my journal and flip through the pages. When I

find what I'm looking for, I pass it to her. She takes it from me and reads it out loud.

"'I need help with the pain. Please do your job.'" She smiles as she hands the journal back to me. "Well, Brooklyn, that's definitely what I'm here for, and today I plan on doing just that."

"That's not me," I fess. "That's Lyric's handwriting."

"I see," she says, folding her hands in her lap. "I think I like Lyric, too. Direct. To the point. And rocking with your best interest in mind. Sounds like a good friend to have."

I fidget with the suede patch on the elbow of my jacket. "Can I tell you something?"

"You can tell me anything."

"Sometimes," I start, lowering my voice to a whisper. "Sometimes it feels like I'm going to crack at any second and then shatter into a bunch of sharp, tiny pieces." I squirm around in the seat and trace my fingers over the velvet arm of the sofa. "Is that weird?"

"I don't think anything you feel is weird, Brooklyn."

The curtains rustle across the room, and I watch them get caught in the Santa Monica breeze.

"Have you ever been really good at something and then something else comes along and suddenly you're not good at it anymore?"

"Of course."

"Like what?" I dig deeper, scooting to the edge of my seat.

"For me it was running track. The older I got, the slower I ran. My feet grew really big one summer, and when I went back to school, I felt like I was running with rocks hanging from my ankles. I was a mess in gym class. And talk about a big blow to my ego! I couldn't believe I didn't have the fastest time anymore." She laughs at herself, and that makes me feel more at ease. She has a soft laugh, and it sticks in my head even after she's done. I decide to share more stuff with her.

"Well, for me it's been selling cookies."

"I have a feeling that this has something to do with Piper Parker coming into the picture?"

"I mean, since she got here, I'm just not having the same kind of success that I'm used to. I just came in third in the race. *Third!*"

"Sounds like she's challenging you. Pushing you to be better."

I twist my face into a scowl. "I wouldn't put it like that, exactly."

"How would you describe it?"

"I don't want to throw her under the bus and sound like I'm just complaining, but the kid is literally stealing my customers. And it's not fair."

"I can see how that would be frustrating."

"And I want to play fair. I want to win the right way. But I don't want to lose the wrong way. And now I don't know what to do." I pick at my cuticle until I see a little speck of blood. "Mom would know what to do. And without her, I'm so confused." I watch the blood trickle over my fingertip and spill onto my jeans.

"You won't always feel like this. Over time, you'll move through the stages of grief and feel new things. We talked about what people go through when they lose someone they love. Do you remember?"

I shrug. I remember some of what she taught me last year that one time I visited with her. But nothing really stuck.

She reaches around her desk and pulls out a pamphlet. She hands it to me and counts on her fingers. "First there's denial, then anger. Bargaining and depression come after that. And finally, there's acceptance."

"I guess I'm stuck in the depression stage because everything reminds me of her and brings me all the way down."

"Sometimes people can jump around from one stage to another; it isn't always linear, you know, in a straight line."

"Dr. Simone?" I slump into my seat.

"Yes, Brooklyn?"

"Sometimes it feels like I'm sinking, being taken down by quicksand. And I can't breathe. And that can't be good. Or healthy either." I slump deeper. "What if I just stop breathing and then I...die? Like my mom."

"I promised to help you with that."

I sit up a little straighter, feeling like all the stuff that I've been pushing down and ignoring is now really important. I've decided: I'm going to make another appointment with her.

"A few quick strategies first," she says, uncrossing her legs. "When you start to feel overwhelmed or like you can't breathe or even when the room starts spinning, I want you to try grabbing your ears and rubbing them, applying pressure up and down your lobe. Press and count to five. Then move lower and count to five." She demonstrates on herself and I imitate her. "And don't forget to breathe."

"Like this?"

She nods. "Yep. The Chinese acupuncturists use needles for the pressure points. This is similar," she says, grinning. "Another thing you can do is simply hold your own hand."

"Okay, now rubbing my ears is one thing, but holding my own hand sounds silly."

"I know," she says, chuckling with me. "But try."

I clasp my hands together. "Now what?"

"Now squeeze and count to five. Then relax." She demonstrates and I follow her lead. "And then do it again. Don't forget to count and to breathe—that's very important."

"How long do I do this?"

"Do it until you start to feel calm, more relaxed. Less anxious."

"Why does this help, Doc?"

"Well, think about when you were little and how safe you felt when you held your mom's or your dad's hand."

"I see," I say, looking down at my hands. "But I don't know about my own hand."

"Okay, okay," she says, letting me off the hook. "I have another one for you since you're great in English. This one might be right up your alley. I want you to start writing down how you feel when you begin to go through this in your mind and in your body." She leans forward and lowers her voice. I can't help but listen harder. I figure she's giving me some important tools. "It really helps to get it out and put it somewhere else. But then I want you to rip that page from your journal and throw it in the trash. The act of tossing the negative, scary thoughts into the trash might help you feel better. That stinkin' thinkin' doesn't belong in your head."

"I can do that."

"Tossing the paper doesn't mean your feelings don't matter. Remember, what you're experiencing is a very real emotional and physical reaction to something that is happening to you. You're healing. Now, I know it doesn't feel like it, but you are. And sometimes healing hurts."

"Like when I have a scab forming and it gets all itchy and even burns sometimes?"

Dr. Simone leans back and smiles. She tugs on her tan blazer, which is unbuttoned over her white button-up, and says, "Exactly."

"*Humph.* I never thought about it that way."

"I've got something else for you today. I'm pretty sure you'll like it due to you being an athlete and all." She stands up and directs me to do the same. "Stand up with me."

I follow her to the light blue wall on the other side of the room. She leans against it and motions for me to lean against it, too.

"What are we doing?" I ask, my eyebrows dancing around my head.

"I know we look silly, but I want you to press your whole body against the wall, really use the strong muscles in those cheer legs and back. Then let the back of your arms press into it, too."

"Okay," I say, pushing backward with all my might. "Now what?"

"Now I want you to count to ten in your head."

"Then what?"

She swipes her hands together, wrapping up the mini lesson. "Then you relax and do it all over again."

Dr. Simone stands next to me and pushes her body into the wall, too. I count aloud, and she counts with me until I'm almost done.

"Eight…nine…and ten!" I yell, and finally exhale. "Whew. I'm pooped."

"Good," she says, wiping her forehead. "I want you to do that every time your heart starts to race and your palms get sweaty and you don't feel like you can breathe."

"And when the room starts to close in on me, too? That only happened once, well, maybe twice, but—"

"Yep, then, too, Brooklyn," she affirms. "I want you to do it three times back-to-back. Don't skip." She lifts her left brow and checks me out. "Got it?"

"Got it," I say, and I mean it.

"And one more thing," she says, very matter-of-fact.

"Yeah?" I ask.

She grins and nods at my journal. "Don't forget to tell Lyric that I did my job."

THIRTEEN

After my session with Dr. Simone, Magic came through on her promise to have us all together at Pink-berry at our favorite table next to the big bay window. Pinkberry is our official headquarters for everything scout squad. And after my therapy session, this was the absolute best way not only to celebrate learning new strategies with Dr. Simone, but also to refocus and get our heads back in the cookie game after coming in third at Friday's tally. After Magic ordered a serious chocolate hazelnut and hung with us for a few, she darted out for a coding sesh with her crew. After that, Lucy put herself in charge and got down to the cookie business at hand. For the past twenty minutes, she's been rambling about how a new way of thinking will change my cookie career.

"I'm preaching the gospel here," Lyric continues as we all lean in with our whole heads. "I mean, we couldn't get anyone to order from us when we knocked on their doors last week." She shrugs. "And don't even get me started on that pop-up store."

Lucy picks the chocolate chips out of her strawberry swirl. "That's because Logan Smith and Piper's cookie truck have really been doing some damage around town. By the time we get to the customer, they're already over it."

"And over us, too," Stella Rose sulks.

"So," Lyric continues, "what I'm saying is that maybe we should think about shifting our strategy to focus on something bigger than grumpy, disloyal customers at home."

"You have something in mind?" I ask, steepling my fingers.

"As a matter of fact, I do!"

I start to get excited as Lyric preps to run down her big plan, but that high energy doesn't last long.

"Look!" Stella Rose points to the flat-screen TV on the wall above the cash register. "Is that... could that... O.M.Goodness grief, it is!"

And right there, on the TV screen, in the middle of

Pinkberry, is Piper Parker's face—in a freaking TELEVI-SION commercial.

"You gotta be kidding me!" Lucy screeches.

"Mercury must be in retrograde," Stella Rose says, wincing.

"She's in an actual TV commercial!" I scream into the air. A few kids look at me and laugh. I ignore them; they have no idea what I'm dealing with right now. "There's no way I can compete with that."

I feel my heart beating so fast and so hard that I think I might pass out in my pomegranate yogurt. And I know what's about to happen next as my palms get clammy and my heartbeat runs around my chest like an Olympian. When I look up at the blurred walls, they're taunting me, threatening to gobble me up. My thoughts are cluttered, but I know Dr. Simone told me to grab ahold of something and then do something else. What was it she told me to do?

Then it hits me...my ears!

I grab them.

Then I grab them harder.

Through the bubbling chaos in my body, I press into the top of my earlobe, remembering to count to five. Then I do it again. But my belly is knotted and my breathing is shallow.

We all gawk at the TV screen, our mouths hanging open, as the spot for Piper's dad's hotel advertises that the Parker will be offering cookies for each of their guests for the rest of the cookie season. Piper's blushing face looks so innocent next to a stack of boxes of Chocolate Marvels and Peanut Butter Babies, but we all know the real deal.

Lyric's words float through the air until they finally land between my eardrums. "You okay, B?"

I shake my head and clasp my hands together before counting to five again. *What's the big deal about the number five anyway?*

I go back and forth between rubbing my ears and holding my own hand until the topsy-turvy parade inside my body finally starts to fizzle out.

"I'm okay," I say to my girls, who are watching me, none of them remembering to blink. "Really, I'm good."

I owe Dr. Simone a gift basket, I think as I glance at the TV screen, which is now showing an ad for solar panels. "I just don't get why the cookie gods have it out for me."

"Is that even fair?" Stella balks. "He has a whole entire hotel that he's going to outfit with cookies. That's a boatload of boxes."

"How does this keep happening?" I whine into the air, watching my cookie queen dreams die a slow death.

"Mercury is definitely in retrograde," Stella Rose confirms, pursing her lips.

After a few minutes of just leering at the TV screen, I finally blurt out, "So now what do we do?"

"We should take this to cookie court," Stella Rose suggests.

Lucy rolls her eyes and brushes her off. "I'm pretty sure that's not a thing."

"Well, it should be," Stella Rose retorts. "None of this is fair."

I cross my legs at the ankles and hold back tears. "I wonder what else she has up her sleeve."

FOURTEEN

"**We have to** one-up her! I can't lose this thing," I say, motoring into my bedroom, my mind racing with so many thoughts about one thing—winning.

"Calm down, B," Lucy says, so sure of herself. "We just need one big stunt to drive this thing home."

"Like what?" I pout. "I don't have her arsenal of weapons to fight back. All I have is...you all."

"Ouch," Lucy says, sucking her teeth. "Harsh much?"

"I didn't mean it that way."

"But we are enough, B," Lyric says, smiling. "We're more than enough."

I turn and check in with Lyric; clearly, I'm missing

something. "Did you just inherit a whole hotel from the Darbys?"

"Even better than that," she says before launching into a song. "See, what I was trying to tell you at Pinkberry Headquarters is that I have a singing voice that can knock this town's socks off."

"Oookay," I say. "But we already know that. You're going to be cast as Dorothy and go on tour one day and take over the world with Blue Ivy." I turn to Lucy and Stella Rose, who both shrug. "What's that got to do with my dismal cookie sales?"

"News flash: You were right when you said that you've got us—because you do. We each bring something special to the table."

"Still not following," I say, throwing my hands in the air.

Stella Rose takes out her camera and starts recording. "I'm not following either, but I do know that sparks fly every time Lyric gets that golden twinkle in her eye."

"See," Lyric continues, pulling me onto the bed with her. "I can sing." Then she points to Stella Rose and nods. "And she can shoot, direct, and edit."

"All facts," says Stella Rose from behind the lens, nodding.

Lucy raises her hand in the air. "Not sure where she's going with this, but I can design my butt off."

Lyric twirls her hands around her head. She's almost as excited as when she decided that a Black Dorothy would set the town on fire. "Look. We have enough talent to reach hundreds, maybe even thousands with the right combo of our gifts. And trust me, it'll be much more exciting and entertaining than a boring old commercial."

We all stop breathing and stare at her. She stares back. Then we're all staring at each other—until she finally reveals, "We're going to make a music video!"

"Ohhh," I sing back to her.

"Was that not clear?" Lyric frowns.

We all shake our heads at her. *Nope.*

"Not even a little," Lucy says, cocking her head to the side and crinkling her brows.

Lyric rolls her eyes at Lucy before turning to me. "Well? What do you think?"

"I'm in," Stella Rose says, standing up to shove her arm into our circle with her palm facing the shaggy throw rug.

"Same," Lucy says, smiling with her whole face as she puts her hand over Stella Rose's.

"B?" they all say, looking at me.

"I think...I think..." I stand, too, and toss my arm into the circle and pile it right on top of theirs. "It's genius!"

"Perf! I'll write a song about B's cookie journey, and we'll make the sickest video to go with it. We can start shooting first thing tomorrow." She's so excited she can barely stand still. I watch her hop to my left and then to my right. "We're gonna need dancers!" she says, pointing to my HoneyBee cheerleading uniform that's hanging on the outside of my closet.

"I can ask the StumbleBees to be our backup dancers." Then I think about it and add, "And maybe they'd even be down to help me with some of the choreography, too. We're definitely going to need cool choreo."

Lucy starts typing so fast it looks like her fingers are dancing around the keyboard, while Stella Rose records it all, never missing a second of this brainstorm. *Our plan is really coming together*, I think as I search around my desk for my phone.

"Let me ask Magic; she's always down for an adventure." When I find the phone, I shoot my fave HoneyBee a text: **What're u doin this weekend?**

"And then by Sunday night, we'll have it all ready so we can post it on social," Lyric belts out, still hopping around my bedroom like an overcaffeinated kangaroo. "I'm going to write the catchiest song so everyone will be singing it Monday morning. I'll make it hard for them to get it out of their heads."

Lucy scoffs. "I hate when that happens."

Stella Rose twirls her scarf around her head. She

always does that when she's in deep thought. "What's the song going to be about?"

"Cookies. Duh." Lucy scrolls through her iPad. "What else would we sing about?"

Lyric scoots to the floor to sit beside Lucy. "We need to be really strategic about our song choice."

I nod back at her. "Indeed." Although I have no idea what she means. How many songs could there be about cookies?

"B's fave group is Girl Power," Lucy says, checking out the music charts on Google. "Let's see what Girl Power's been doing lately."

"Oh. Oh! *Oh!*" I yelp, jumping up and down. "Girl Power's debut song, 'Monster'—it's a classic."

"I heart that song," Stella Rose says, falling back onto the bed. "My favorite part is when she says,

> *I'm your favorite monster.*
> *No, not an impostor.*
> *I'll make you really lovesick*
> *Till you call the doctor.*

"I dig that part, too!" Lyric bobs her head, grabbing a pencil from my desk. She flicks it in the air to the beat in her head. "Let's remix the whole song. We can call it—"

"'Cookie Monster,'" I giggle, and pull up Girl Power's song on YouTube.

"That's not funny," Lyric says, singing along with the start of the Girl Power song. "It's actually really brillz."

"And brand aligned," Betty Jean says as she passes in the hallway.

I grab my hairbrush and dance in the mirror, belting out the new lyrics.

> *I'm your cookie monster.*
> *No, not an impostor.*
> *I'll keep your cookies comin'.*

We all start to giggle, and then Betty Jean pokes her head in the bedroom and sings.

> *Sell them by the dozen.*

"That's a fab start," Lyric says, still bobbing her head. "But I'll play around with it and see what else I can come up with."

"Cool beans," Lucy says. "The rest of us can start thinking about the music video."

"Lobster. Mobster." Lyric's thoughts are racing all around the room. "What other words rhyme with *monster*?"

"Helicopter?" I offer.

"Hmm." Lyric taps the pencil on her forehead. "No worries, I'll figure it out. You stick to the choreography until I need your voice in a few." She checks her phone. "I'm going to run down the street and be back in a sec with some stuff to record."

"Like now?" I shriek.

"Like, yes!" Lyric shrieks back. "When you're on fire, you really shouldn't stop the momentum. And, people," she yells into the air, "we're on fire!"

"Okay," I say. "We'll figure out the video."

"BRB." Lyric bolts toward the front door as Stella Rose suggests spots to hit up for the video.

I ball my fist and wave it in the air, snickering, "We're going to make a smash!"

Lucy and Stella Rose are working with me on some pretty basic choreo when Lyric bolts back into my bedroom with a duffel bag slung over her shoulder. She hoists it onto my bed and exhales. "I think I brought everything."

I pad over to the bed, and my eyebrows shoot into my hairline. "What's all that stuff? I thought you were just going home to grab two microphones for you and me to sing into."

"You need more than a microphone, B, if you're going

to make a hit." She opens the bag and pulls out some serious recording equipment.

"What's this?" I hold up a round thing that looks like a Nerf ball.

"That's a pop filter." She pulls out more stuff until she finds a pair of jumbo headphones. I bend down so she can put them over my head. "You'll need these. We also have a few speakers and monitors and cables in there, too."

"Holy macaroni!" Stella Rose yelps.

"This digital audio workstation is my baby; that's going to do most of the work for us to get our song ready."

"You came ready with the heat," Lucy says, snapping her fingers.

"B's bedroom is a total recording studio." Stella Rose's eyes pop as she marvels at the setup.

Lyric steps back to admire her work. "And voilà! We're ready to record."

After a few unsuccessful attempts, my voice finally hits all the notes, belting out our song like a pro—well, close enough.

I sit in my chair and swivel it around a few times until I'm dizzy. "I can't believe we just recorded a song. Like, a real live song!"

"We're officially the Cookie Monsters now," Stella Rose says.

Lucy rubs her belly and moans, "Now I want cookies."

"Can I hear it?" Betty Jean asks, popping into the room, anticipation all over her face.

"That'll be the true test," Lyric says, adjusting the equipment. "If Betty Jean loves it and can't get it out of her head, then we did our jobs."

The song starts, and right away Betty Jean wriggles her butt around in the air. In no time, she has the chorus down. "That *is* catchy," she says, and sings.

> *I'm your cookie monster.*
> *No, not an impostor.*
> *I'll keep your cookies comin'.*
> *Sell them by the dozen.*

I high-five Lyric, who fist-bumps Stella Rose. Lucy and Betty Jean hip-bump to the beat. We all giggle into the air and I can't help but wish Mom were here to see this. She'd get such a kick out of it all, and I just know she'd be singing her heart out, too.

But this is just the beginning.

With only two weeks left in cookie season, it's time to get busy shooting the coolest video *ever*!

I glance at my girls circling the room, singing our new

song. I have to make the world forget about Piper Parker and her food truck, her sales team, and now her big fat commercial.

And I'm willing to do whatever it takes to make that happen.

FIFTEEN

It's Saturday morning, and my bedroom looks like it's been transformed into one of the dressing rooms backstage at the Kids' Choice Awards. My scout squad bustles around, taking turns standing in the mirror, modeling our custom Lucy's Looks costumes, made especially for the "Cookie Monster" music video.

"I really like that blingy vest with the matching *QUEEN* snapback on you," Lucy says to me, pointing to the embellishment. "The retro green joggers with the sequins symmetrically sewn down the side are *every*thing."

She's right, too, I think, sticking out my leg and waving my hand down my side. Lucy put her heart into designing all of our outfits last night. "I didn't sleep a wink," she kept repeating to us all morning over orange juice and blueberry bagels. It paid off, though: Every detail is purrr-fect and now we look like true scout superstars.

"I'm in love," Stella Rose says, pulling up her bedazzled pants, which match mine. "These joggers should be in your shop."

"Don't think I haven't thought of that already!" Lucy blushes, flipping her newly colored purple hair over her shoulder while I pose in the mirror.

"So, which scout are you?" Stella Rose asks. "Tomboy scout?"

"Why does everything have to always involve boys?" I ask, standing up straight to face her. "Just call me sporty scout."

Lucy nods at me and snaps a picture with her very professional camera. She said she was going to use our pics for the digital portfolio on her website. I don't blame her; our costumes are killer.

Lucy turns to Stella Rose and hands her a pair of nerdy retro eyeglasses. "Put these on. They complete your look."

"But I'm already wearing my own glasses," she says.

"They don't really relay the vibe."

"And what vibe is that?" Stella Rose asks, checking herself out in the mirror.

"B is sporty scout and you're... well, you're nerdy scout," Lucy says, shrugging. "Makes sense to me."

"How about we call me techie scout instead? I don't like the connotation that *nerd* carries."

"Sure," Lucy says, shoving her left hand into her hip. "Whatever it takes to get you to put these glasses on and pose for your shot."

Stella Rose pushes the glasses up her nose and flips her long pigtails with the big, barreled curls over her shoulder. "Okay, I'm ready for my picture," she says, snapping the green-and-brown-checkered suspenders over her polo shirt. She grins into the camera. "I could really get into these."

"The matching bow tie is my fave," Lyric says, pulling her socks over her knee to polish off her sassy scout look. She stands up and tugs at the green-and-brown-pleated miniskirt, which is the same as Lucy's. Then she poofs her blond Afro as big as it'll go. "And my rock star hair is wicked!"

"What kind of scout are you supposed to be?" Stella Rose asks Lucy, who's outfitted in everything blingy— from her hair bows and eyebrows down to her shoelaces. "I'm fashion scout, of course."

I spin around when I hear the doorbell. "Our backup dancers are here!"

"Perfect timing," Lucy says, grabbing up their hair bows and necklaces from the bed.

I skip down the hall and swing open the door to see Magic in her HoneyBee cheer uniform.

"Hiya, B," she says, shaking her butt and beatboxing between rapping. "It's time to get our dance on!"

I look past my favorite HoneyBee and see Winnie and LuLu beaming back at me. I can't help but squeal, "The Stumbles! You guys actually came!"

"Wouldn't miss it for the world," Winnie says, batting her lashes at me from her decorated wheelchair. "You love it, don't you? I know you do!" She points to the wheels with green, pink, and red coverings. "You said this was the color scheme for the shoot."

"Are those cookies sewn into the fabric on top of your spokes?" I swoon at both her creativity and her commitment to the branding. "You're literally rolling on cookies. Thanks, Winn." I watch her perfect a 360-degree spin on her back wheels, then I bend down and hug them both, whispering, "What would I do without my cheer squad?"

I step back and add, "Thanks for sending over the video of the dance routine. Now that we all know the steps and the song is ah-may-zing, it's time to get to it." I stop and count each of us on the porch. Then I look back at the pink Caddy—then back at all *seven* of us. "How are we all going to fit in that?" I ask, stumped. "I don't think we thought this through."

And right on cue, Betty Jean pulls in front of the house in a black Sprinter van, rolling down the window. She beeps the horn three times and yells, "Are my super-stars ready?"

"That's us?!" Lucy geeks, pointing to the cool ride with the blacked-out windows. "Betty Jean! You're—"

"The best troop leader ever!" I yell, running to the curb.

We scramble to the van and load in before heading to the Pier with "Cookie Monster" playing on repeat. By the time Betty Jean pulls over on Ocean Ave, we're yelling every word of our new song out the windows at all the passersby. And whenever anyone waves at us, we giggle and then hyperwave right back.

Not five minutes later, we're making a beeline for the carnival at the end of the Pier, grabbing tickets so we can film on the rides. We hop on the Ferris wheel, waving at the Stumbles on the ground, as the ride takes us away. They shrink into tiny dots the farther toward heaven we climb. I take a sec to appreciate how much cooler Santa Monica looks from this top spot in the sky. The sparkly ocean seems to stretch for miles, straight into the horizon. I blissfully sigh.

"Okay, Lyric," Stella Rose says, snapping me out of awe when the ride comes to a full stop. She balances the camera and directs us like a pro. "Start the song on your phone, and let's get our footage before this thing moves again. It's…showtime!"

We hear the first beat, and Stella Rose shoves the camera in my face as I sing along. I wave my arms around and bop my head especially hard when it gets to the chorus. I watch as Stella Rose masterfully pans the camera around to the Pacific Ocean. She makes sure to get shots of the surfers riding the waves before swinging back around to us. We belt the lyrics like it's a live performance.

"Cut!" She lowers the camera and announces to the world, "That was poetic. Rapturous. Divine. Ethereal."

"You got what we need?" Lyric asks as Stella Rose double-checks the footage.

"Okay, let's do another take just to be on the safe side." Stella Rose peers through the camera lens and flashes a thumbs-up. Lyric, obeying the bat signal, starts the music, and we take it from the top.

When we're done, the ride swings around to the other side of Santa Monica. "That was premium stuff!" Stella Rose twists in her seat and pans the camera toward town. The houses on the boardwalk, the tiny people on the Pier, and, of course, the waves smashing against the shore all get their moment to shine in the imaginary spotlight.

"This is just for an establishing shot," she boasts. "A really great establishing shot."

When the ride finally stops to let us off, we race to the roller coaster.

"Let's split up into two cars," Lucy says as we hop on the ride. "I'll ride with Lyric so Stella Rose can record B."

We fasten our seat belts and take turns singing into the camera until the coaster takes off, whipping us around to the left and then to the right and then up a hill and then back down.

"Whoa!" I screech to Stella Rose, between yelling out the lyrics. "Are you getting it?"

Lyric yells back from the coaster seat behind me and Stella Rose, "Just keep singing!"

"Love your facials," Stella Rose screams over the wind.

My hair is braided on both sides with my thick curls parted into a fauxhawk on top of my head, which would be really fresh if it weren't blowing into my eyes. I try to pretend that everything's just fine, even though I can't see a thing and my hair keeps getting stuck to my front teeth.

Stella Rose films as the coaster whizzes around a curve and makes its final climb up the last hill.

"Hold on. I'm shooting the final drop," she explains to us. "I need you guys to sing the chorus for this part. It'll be an awesome aerial shot."

We throw our hands into the air and sing our hearts out.

> *I'm your cookie monster.*
> *No, not an impostor.*
> *I'll keep your cookies comin'.*
> *Sell them by the dozen.*

She turns to me, and I yell:

> *Sell them by the dozen.*

"So cool," Lucy yelps when the coaster comes to a screeching stop.

"Whew! Are we done?" I wring my hands in the air. "Because I'm pooped and that was kinda scary. Definitely not doing it again."

Stella Rose checks out some of the footage and nods. "It's in the can!" she yells, packing her camera into her bag. "That's a wrap on the Pier."

"You're a real pro, girl," Lyric says to Stella Rose as we head to the beach to join the StumbleBees, who are chasing each other around barefoot, playing in the water, and kicking up wet sand.

Winnie grips a Super Soaker water gun that I'm pretty sure belongs to one of the boys making a sandcastle by the shoreline, and I do my best to stay out of her way.

"There's nowhere to run, nowhere to hide," Winnie chuckles, shooting everyone in sight, getting them more and more drenched.

Stella Rose rushes to grab her camera from her bag and starts recording. She captures the water fight, and by the time the Stumbles realize that she's filming, they're soaked. We're in stitches, grabbing our bellies and laughing so hard we can't catch our breath.

"Guys! Wait!" I screech. "Now you'll be all soggy for the shoot."

"But it's going to look so cool," Stella Rose explains. "You'll love the visuals, B; just trust me."

"Okay, but don't frizz my 'fro," I say, covering my fauxhawk. "Betty Jean worked on it all morning."

Stella Rose shoots me a thumbs-up, and after several run-throughs of the song with the choreography, we notice a small group of people surrounding us.

An older lady and her gray-haired husband applaud after we finish the final take. One little girl who resembles a boy taking pics of the sandcastle even comes up to ask for a selfie.

"Told you this whole song and dance was going to be a smash," Lyric says. "First you get the kids hooked, then you get the moms, then the rest of the world falls in line."

"And just wait until we drop this video tomorrow. I'm going to stay up all night past lights-out and edit this baby," Stella Rose boasts. "Piper Parker won't know what hit her."

After the last shot is captured, we load back into Betty Jean's black superhero van, still excited, and on top of the world. Each of us takes turns blabbing on and on about the pure epicness of shooting at two of my fave spots—the Pier and the beach. We talk over each other, reliving every minute of the day, thrilled to be making art.

Betty Jean drops us off in front of Pinkberry, and we rush to line up on the Promenade, ready for our first shot in our new location. I try to ignore all the people who are bustling through the shopping complex, going in and out of all the cool stores.

The Stumbles line up in front of the pretzel shop, and Magic nods to let us know they're all set. A few couples and an old man with a huge cinnamon pretzel start to form a semicircle around us, waiting to see what we have up our sleeves. I can't take my eyes off the pretzel, and now I want a snack.

"Cue the music," Stella Rose says to Lyric, and motions for the dancers to start the routine. I try to refocus and muddle through the first verse, causing Stella Rose to wince.

"Cut!" she yells after Magic does a series of spins to start the chorus.

"That was the first cousin to flawless," Stella Rose announces. "B, uh—"

"I know, I know. My stomach is gurgling," I spout back at her. "I need a snack."

"No, it's not you," she says before clearing her throat a few times and bobbing her head in the direction of the Verizon store across the street. That's when I spy Piper Parker and her entourage making fun of us in the distance. Piper points to Winnie and giggles, then to Magic, and then to the rest of us. Her hyena cackles bounce off the waffle stand behind her. Then, when she's all laughed out, she turns away and parades down the street with her crew of meanies in her shadow, all mocking our dance sequence.

"Ignore her. You're going to be a cookie sensation," Magic says, grabbing my hand. "I've never done anything this major before." Her eyes go wide, and she takes a really deep breath. "You're making an actual *music* video. How amazy is that?! And Piper Parker doesn't know anything; you'll always be our cookie queen."

The rest of the Stumbles nod in agreement, and Magic's face brightens more than a few shades.

"Piper has no idea," Lucy says, snarling at the entourage of venom in the distance. "What we're about to drop is going to rock this town."

Lyric folds her arms over her chest, and we all get back in formation to finish the scene. "Now, let's hurry up and get this in the can because I'm with B—I desperately need a venti hot chocolate."

A mom with two little girls and a stroller walks past us. She gives Stella Rose a five-dollar bill. "You girls are awesome. Let me know when your single comes out. My daughters love it."

"And now I want to be sporty scout for Halloween," one of the little girls in a frilly dress and patent leather shoes professes. Her mother smiles as she pulls the little girl away.

"Okay." Her mom winks back at us. "Sporty scout it is."

"See, it's like I told you," Lyric says, handing me the five-dollar bill. "First you get the kids, then you get the moms, then the rest of the world falls in line."

SIXTEEN

I counted down the hours, and now it's finally time!

We're all seated at our usual table by the big window at Pinkberry, bubbling over. I'm on pins and needles, so enjoying my pomegranate swirl isn't exactly at the top of my list right now. Even my taste buds must be ready for the big music video reveal because, after a few scoops, the blueberries started to taste like raisins—and I absolutely hate raisins, almost as much as I hate getting the flu shot every year.

Stella Rose whirls her mango yogurt around the cup. She picks at the toasted almonds and stares at her laptop. "Okay. Is everyone ready?"

"C'mon! Just post it! I don't think I can wait another second," Lucy pipes, staring at the Instagram page with our video frozen in place. "We've been waiting all day for this life-changing moment."

Lyric stabs her chocolate chips into the strawberry yogurt and announces, "This is going to be epic!"

"Okay, B, you can press the magic button," Stella Rose says, pointing to the small keypad on her phone. Then she rubs her hands together feverishly and says, "Be good to us, Insta."

"Let's all do it together," I offer, huddling closer to my squad. "I didn't make this happen on my own."

One by one, we hang our index fingers over her cell.

"Ready. Set…" Stella Rose signals, her eyes darting around the table from one pensive smile to the next.

"Go!" I say, biting into my bottom lip, as we send the music video file straight into the stratosphere.

Lyric takes a deep breath, her chest deflating, as all the air escapes from her lungs. "There's no turning back now."

One by one, we sit back in our plastic seats—and we wait. Stella Rose twirls her mulberry cashmere scarf around her fingertips while Lyric keeps refreshing my page—over and over. And over.

"That's not going to generate views, ya know," Lucy snarks at her, sucking her teeth.

Lyric taps her bedazzled nails on the table. "What do you suggest we do? Stella Rose is going to choke herself with that scarf."

"Wait! I almost forgot," Stella Rose says, swiping through her phone—back and forth and then back again. "I have a few hashtags I wanted to add, like 'hashtag TheCookieMonster.'"

"And don't forget to link my Virtual Cookie app in my bio," I say, snapping my fingers.

"I'm putting the Virtual Cookie website link in the bio right now so IG can drive traffic right back to the order form and people can buy, buy, buy!" Stella Rose says, typing a million miles a minute. "And on Facebook and Tik-Tok, too, of course."

"Looks like we're all set," I say, nodding at the cell in the center of the table.

I wait as long as I can, but when nobody likes or views the video, I yell, "C'mon!"

I flop my arms around the air above my coily fauxhawk, waiting for someone—anyone—to check out our masterpiece.

"You gave it, like, five seconds. This stuff takes time," Lucy chastises, trying to keep me calm.

"She's right, there's a whole algorithm in place," Lyric agrees. "And we have to respect the algorithm."

"Uh-huh," I grimace, nibbling on my nail beds. "Sure. Respect the algorithm."

"That's right," Lyric says, tugging at the mesh sleeve of her black crop top. "We're in too deep not to."

"But what if no one cares?" I sulk, faster than I can catch myself.

Stella Rose tightens her grip on her scarf. "Or even worse, what if no one watches?"

I gnaw on my cuticles, and then the most brillz idea pops into my head. "Now, I know this sounds like a long shot, maybe even a fit of delirium, but just hear me out."

"We're listening," Lyric says, cupping her earlobe.

"What if we tagged Girl Power. I mean, it *is* their song."

"You *are* delirious!" Lucy spouts. "Why would they ever care about—"

"Done!" Stella Rose says, shrugging.

"You didn't!" I exclaim.

Stella Rose shrugs again. "It can't hurt." She turns to reassure me and then grins at Lucy. "Seriously. It can't hurt, can it?"

For the next five minutes, we sit at our table, refreshing the Insta page over and over, until I can't take it anymore.

"We need a distraction," I say after a few somber minutes with *zero* views.

"I have the perfect one," Lucy says, grabbing Stella Rose's laptop. "Where's your submission video? You know, the one for the documentary you told B you were filming?"

"Oh. Uh," Stella Rose stalls. "I, uh..."

"What's with the extra-long pause?" Lyric asks, narrowing her eyes at Stella Rose.

"It's just not ready yet," she answers, her focus darting around the room.

We all eye Stella Rose, wondering what's up with her hesitation to show us what she's been working on.

"Uh-huh," Lucy finally says, flipping through all the open tabs on Stella Rose's computer.

"It's not there," Stella Rose finally admits. "Actually, I kind of stopped working on it."

"You what?" Lucy balks, moving through all her files in her documents folder. "And why would you do that? You've been completely consumed with it."

"It's no big deal."

"Uh, yeah it is!" Lyric says. "You've been shoving that cam in B's face every chance you get, catching all the delish cookie moments."

"She caught a case of the butterflies," I say, trying to explain gently.

"What's that even mean?" Lucy barks at Stella Rose. Fast fact: She can be pretty impatient. And today is no

180

different. "This was very important to you, and so now it's important to us, too."

And it's at this exact moment that my heart aches for my friend. I know she didn't upload a video because of her own anxiety. It's a real thing, and it comes in many shapes and sizes.

"I've been struggling to record the intro part of the video—and it's mandatory. So I just thought that maybe this wasn't the right competition for me."

Lyric and Lucy back down when Stella Rose's hands get shaky and her cheeks blush red as she wipes the sweat beads from her upper lip. When she struggles to regain her composure, I lean over and clasp my hands together under the table. I nudge her, nodding at my hands, urging her to do the same. When she does, I whisper in her ear, "Now squeeze while you slowly count to five. And do that three times. Don't skip."

When she imitates me, I explain, "It's a little anxiety hack, courtesy of Dr. Simone. Maybe it'll help."

I massage her back gently as she moves her lips, silently counting to five.

Lucy's neck stretches over my shoulder, studying my phone as I keep refreshing. "But farealz, what if no one sees it?"

Lyric crosses her arms over her chest. "Are you kidding

me?" she scoffs. "That video is fab! We did an amazy job, and soon enough, everyone will be hyping us to do a whole album."

"I sure hope so," I utter, feeling doubtful that the video will supercharge my cookie career.

Lyric pulls her phone from its crocheted holder dangling from her neck. She punches in a few words. Then she punches in a few more. "There." She sits back in her chair and exhales. "It's done."

"What did you do?" My eyes flicker with hope, mostly because she has that look on her face that she gets when she's about to challenge Mr. Chang about her grade on one of his infamous pop quizzes. Determination!

"I did what I should've done in the beginning."

"And...?" we all ask, waiting for the big reveal.

"I asked my mom to repost the video."

We all gasp, staring at her like she just stepped up to be the next seventh-grade presidential candidate. As her words land softly on my heart, I reach for her shoulder and rest my hand on it.

"But she never got back to you last time when she was in Boston. Or Baltimore. Or—"

"Yeah, but this involves music. It's right up her alley." Lyric grins at the synergy. "Before, selling scout cookies wasn't exactly a good fit for her socials, but now, this might be more on brand for her."

"Music *is* her world," Stella Rose says, nodding in total agreement.

"And tell her that I'm donating ten percent of my sales to the Our House Grief Support Center in Los Angeles."

"You're what?"

"Yep. I mean, some of those kids don't have a Dr. Simone. And losing someone you love isn't easy to get through without help."

"I'm adding that to the caption," Stella Rose says as she types into her phone.

Lucy checks me out while Lyric just shakes her head. "You never stop amazing me, my friend," she says before sending off a text update to her mom.

And then we wait. And we wait some more—until Lyric's phone dings.

We all freeze.

Could this be the one big break I need to send my music video soaring through the World Wide Web?

"Is that her?" Lucy checks to see.

"What'd she say?" I inch to the edge of my seat. "Is she going to repost it?"

"Well..." Lyric starts reading and then...she just

sighs. "She said she'll check it out later. She's in band rehearsal right now. In Atlanta." Lyric turns to face me. "But she sends her congrats to you for doing something so cool."

"I guess that's something," I say. "Right?"

Lyric hangs her head and taps her foot on the tiled floor. "I just wish she was more available." Then she stops and sits up straight, fixing her face to show that she's perfectly okay with her mom being too busy for her. Then she says it, those words we've all come to expect when she's down in the dumps but she wants to convince us otherwise. "I'm good. It's all good. Everything's good." She looks up from her phone, and we all reluctantly nod back at her.

"Have you ever thought about telling her exactly how you feel?" Stella Rose whisper-asks.

"I do tell her." The corners of Lyric's mouth drop into a scowl. "I just did—in that text."

"Well, not exactly," Lucy disagrees. "You asked her for something. Maybe follow that up by letting her know just how important stuff is to you, like you just told us."

"What she's doing is far more important than anything I could ever want. You have to understand the music biz; it's pretty demanding." Lyric turns her head to the big window and stares out of it. "I want to be just like her when I grow up, only maybe I'll make more time for my daughter."

"You matter, too," I say, trying not to upset her. "You're twelve. And you need stuff. So, like, maybe if you tried expressing what you need from her, she'd be more available."

"So...what are you suggesting?"

"Well, Dr. Simone tells me to write everything down. Maybe you could write down how you're feeling and then give it to her."

Stella Rose points to her phone. "Or send it to her, like in an email."

Lucy's brows dance around her head while she ponders our latest conundrum. Then she adds, "Or even a text. That could work, too."

Lyric slumps deeper into her chair and starts stabbing at the chocolate chips in her cup. "I don't know. I probably shouldn't bug her."

"Dr. Simone says we have to be able to share how we're feeling, and writing it down is the least scary way of all."

"I'm not scared," Lyric bites back at us. "That's dumb. She's my mom."

"Good," Lucy says, grabbing her iPad and opening a fresh email. "Then try typing a few lines and see how you feel."

But when Lyric doesn't budge, Lucy begins typing for her.

Dear Mom,

"I wouldn't start it that way," Lyric says, sucking her teeth.

"Then type whatever you—"

Lucy stops talking when an email notification flashes onto the screen—from *her* mom.

"OMG!" Lucy shrieks as she reads the short note. "Crud!"

"What happened, Luce?" I ask, looking over her shoulder to read her mom's very stern words.

> Get home right now! Who bought all
> this stuff? And how did you pay for this?
> You have some explaining to do. And so
> does your sister!

"*No!*" Lucy covers her mouth with her hand. "She found the Amazon shipment of stuff for my accessories."

Stella Rose leans over, too, taking a closer look at the words. "I thought your sister was going to sign for it."

Lucy shrugs. "I dunno. Maybe she wasn't there to intercept the delivery."

"What did your mom say?" I point to the screen.

"I have to get home." Lucy moves faster than I've ever seen. "Double crud!"

"Lucy," Lyric begins as Lucy tosses her iPad into her backpack. "What would happen if you told your mom exactly how *you* feel? You know, told her how important your shop is to you?"

"I see what you're doing." Lucy wriggles her finger around in the air. "Don't try to turn this around on me."

"She does have a point, Luce," I say. "It might actually help."

"You don't understand. My parents aren't like yours. They're super serious about my career in…in…in…"

"Medicine!" Lyric snaps. "See, you can't even say the word. That's how much you detest the very idea."

"Facts," I say, snapping my fingers. "Looks like Lyric's not the only one who needs to have a heart-to-heart with the parentals."

"Just think about it. Both my parents came to this country with nothing but the clothes on their backs. They tell me this story every time I start a new school year. They didn't have anything. And they made a life for themselves and worked overtime to put themselves through college. They only want what's best for me, and the way they see it, becoming a doctor will make their struggles all worth it."

"But that's not what *you* want," I say, tugging on her elbow. When she pulls away, I don't fight her. I know when to back off. And now is that exact time!

"They've sacrificed everything for me. Even though it's not what I want, it's what I need—to make them happy." Lucy zips her backpack and heads for the door. "I gotta go. Pray that I don't get put on punishment for the rest of my life."

Stella Rose and I make the sign of the cross.

Lyric reaches for her phone and pulls up an empty email.

" 'Dear Mom,' " she starts.

Stella Rose nods at me with a sparkle in her eyes that says it's all going to work out, and I'm filled with hope that someone at this table will get what they deserve today. And it's perfectly okay that it's not me.

SEVENTEEN

I shuffle into homeroom Monday morning feeling a lot less confident than I did before we uploaded the video.

"What's got you so down?" Lyric asks as I slide into my desk in the middle of the room.

"Have you checked the views? The likes? The comments?" I shake my head and pout. "And don't even get me started on my sales—or the fact that I barely have any new ones since the music video dropped."

"I've been totally preoccupied with it, too," Lyric cosigns. "More than I was before my last audition for the winter festival."

"How am I going to use the video to advertise my cookies if no one ever sees it?"

"I know it's scary, but we put our best foot forward, so I'm choosing to believe that it'll work out just the way it's supposed to."

I shrug deeper into my desk.

"Don't worry, B; we'll make a strong comeback before Friday's tally. You'll see. I know it's not a huge jump, but your views and likes are climbing." She swipes through a few apps until she lands on Virtual Cookie. "And your sales numbers are—"

"I checked it before class," I say, shrugging again. "Nothing exciting happening there."

Lyric shows me her phone. "You made over thirty sales since it went live."

"Seriously?! I don't know how that happened. When I checked it this morning, there were only ten new orders. And don't even let me get started on Insta." I pull out my phone and check Instagram. Seven views. *Seven!* And only seven likes, too. *Seven!* I shove the phone under Lyric's nose, rattling off the names:

1. Betty Jean—@CurlsnPearlssalon
2. Lyric—@yourfaverockstar4life
3. Stella Rose—@wheresmycamera12

4. Dad—@Samsdadworld
5. Betty Jean's assistant—@CurlsnPearls2assistant
6. Brooklyn Ace—@aceof_scoutcookies
7. Random Woman—@getyourfollowersup

"Get your followers up? Seriously?!" I glare down at my phone. "My sales numbers are moving like a turtle," I say in my most whiny voice, paddling my hands in front of my nose in slow motion. "And I want to be the hare."

Lyric tries to hold back her laughter. I try to rally and regroup, but it's impossible when I spy Piper waltzing into the room, flanked by her girl-groupies, Rachel and Lindsay. She's holding a big neon-yellow box in her arms, completely unbothered, and smiling at everyone as the rest of her entourage rushes in on the heels of her snake-skin boots. I blink hard, secretly wishing the dead reptile would come back to life to slink around her legs and cut off all circulation. I know that's not nice, but I never said I was perfect.

"I bet those boots are real," Lyric whispers into my ear. "She's the kind of girl who'd kill an innocent animal in the name of fashion."

"She's coming this way," I say, bracing myself. I shove my hands into the front pocket of my CARPE DIEM hoodie.

"Hi, Brooklyn," Piper says, handing the box to Rachel.

Piper fluffs the puffy sleeves on her purple cotton mini-dress and then looks me up and down.

"Hi," I respond as dryly as possible and cock my head to the side—but even sideways she looks like a giant anaconda.

"I saw your music video." She shrugs and tosses her long, distressed braid over her shoulder. "Cute."

I roll my eyeballs into the back of my head and mumble, "Thanks."

"But there were a few things I would've done differently." She's towering over me in her heels and doesn't mind one bit that she's looking down on me. "You're kind of talented. Too bad your special gifts will be all for nothing. Nobody cares to watch you and your crew dancing around town, singing about scout cookies—especially Girl Power."

"Huh?" I squawk.

"Stop tagging them in your posts; it makes you look ridiculous. And thirsty."

"And desperate," Rachel says over Piper's shoulder.

One by one, the kids in the room stop bantering with each other and turn to watch our heated sideshow.

Piper, realizing that she has an audience, leans down and slams her hand onto my desk, causing me to flinch—and I hate it when I flinch.

"They'd never respond to a nobody like you anyway," she says.

That's when I spy Logan Smith and Dallas Chase, the superstar quarterback at Valentine Middle, sidle up to us.

"You're a total nobody! An absolute nobody! A *complete* nobody!!" Rachel yells into the air.

"Is all that necessary?" Dallas challenges Rachel, digging his hands into the pockets of his Valentine varsity jacket. "C'mon. She's somebody. She's Brooklyn Ace."

"And you're Piper Parker," Logan adds.

Dallas points to Lyric. "And she's Lyric Darby. See, we're all somebody. No need to throw insults around."

"Mind your own beeswax," Piper snips at the athletes, not caring that they've been working for her for *free* for the past two weeks.

The class quiets, all eyes focused solely on us now. I don't think I'm even breathing when Dallas steps closer to Piper and says, "This *is* my beeswax, especially if we're the top sellers on your team."

"Who says I even need you? You're not that special."

"Whoaaaa!" the class erupts, then scatters to their seats when Ms. Pepper, our homeroom teacher, walks into the room.

"Have it your way," Logan says, eyeing Dallas as they walk toward their seats, too. "We're out."

I'm in shock and awe that they had my back. If I had to bet, I would've put all my money on them accepting the big cookie prizes, standing right by Piper Parker's side. Logan Smith stole all my Old Faithfuls, for crying out loud. But when Dallas flashes me a sincere smile and Logan tosses me a thumbs-up, it's becoming clear that I would've lost my life savings on that bet.

Piper nudges my pencil to the edge of my desk and then pushes it over. "You're going to have to step your game up if you want to compete with me."

Lyric sucks her teeth and stomps her vegan open-toe booties into the linoleum floor.

"I'm not worried," I lie, trying not to let my twitching lip tell on me.

"You should be," she says, slithering away with her minions by her side.

"Two minutes until the bell," Ms. Pepper states, gathering the papers on her desk. "Everyone, get settled so we can run through today's housekeeping."

Lyric grabs my hand, and I stare at my high-top Reeboks. "She's underestimating me and it's driving me bananas," I say. My right foot dangles feverishly around my ankle like it's about to snap straight off. "We can't let her win."

"Don't freak out," Lyric says, smoothing out the gray

tulle on her skirt, which is layered over her houndstooth leggings. She holds the netting in place and squeezes into her desk. "We won't. We'll take her down from that high horse—trust me."

Lyric puts her hand over my knee and applies pressure. She nods emphatically at my foot that's still flying around—right along with my anxiety, which is definitely getting the best of me. I take a lonnng, deep breath and exhale slowly while frantically massaging my earlobes.

"We just need to give it some time." Lyric bends over to pick up my pencil. "People will love the song and the video so much that they'll be forced to buy your cookies 'cause, well, you're the official cookie monster."

My eyes dart around the classroom. Everyone is staring at me, except Logan and Dallas, who are deep in a private convo that no one else can hear. A few seconds pass before I spy them bump fists into a secret handshake. Then they glance back at me, causing me to look away.

"'Kay," I mutter back at Lyric. I cross my fingers and close my eyes, wishing for her words to become gospel and my music video to blow all the way up!

I open my eyelids when I feel a tap on my shoulder.

"Uh…yeah?" I say when I see Logan and Dallas standing over me.

"We were talking," Dallas starts.

"And we saw your video," Logan says, nodding like he's staring at a double cheeseburger.

"And, dude, it was way cool," Dallas finishes, like he's fantasizing about that same burger, too, but with extra pickles.

"Yeah?" I say, glancing down at my phone to peek at my Insta:

99 views

67 likes

Wait.

Make that…

74 likes

"Told you," Lyric says when I look up and see others in the class holding their phones, pointing at me, smiling with what looks like approval on their faces, too.

Logan sits in the seat beside me. "We like how you're moving around social, and we just wanted to say that if you're interested, we'd consider joining your sales team."

"Yes! She's interested!" Lyric belts out before I can finish processing what they've said. "She's definitely interested!"

"You can count us both in," Dallas says, playing with the zipper on his black-and-gold jacket. "And a few others, too. There's a cool buzz going around the school about you. We can help with that."

"Are you serious?" I blink hard. And then again. "I mean...cool."

"Yeah," Logan explains. "We love your song and your video. That was the freshest chess move we've seen since this cookie thing started."

"And you're sure?" I whisper-ask, leaning toward them. "You want to be on *my* team?"

"Absolutely!" Dallas says, shoving a V, the Valentine symbol we make at all the games, in front of my face. "You have two weeks left to turn this thing around and get your sales numbers up."

Logan blows on his knuckles and rubs them over his chest. "And we can help you make that happen."

"Okay," I say, not about to turn down a few assists from the most popular boys in school. Then I think about it for another second. "And you're positive that you don't want to be on her team anymore?"

Logan folds his arms over his chest. "Let's just say we'd rather not be associated with conceit and arrogance."

"Plus you're really nice, and we think it's cool that

you're donating a percentage of your sales to the kids at the Grief Center."

I exhale with relief as Ms. Pepper takes off her pumpkin cardigan and pushes her sleeves over her elbows. This is our cue to pay attention while she sits at her very organized desk and reads the day's announcements from the paper on top of her laptop. We listen to her rattle off several school reports about clubs and sports, and when she's done, she asks, "Does anyone have anything they'd like to share with us today?"

Heads turn, and we all wait for the usual hands to shoot into the air. I fidget around in my seat when I hear Piper say, "Actually, I need to address the class this morning. I have something to share that I think will be of interest."

"Go ahead, Ms. Parker," Ms. Pepper says, standing. "We're listening."

The class turns to Piper, who walks to the front of the room with the big yellow box. "These are from the Cupcake Concierge," she says, opening the lid. "I brought these in for the class because everyone has been so welcoming and nice to me since I started at Valentine. Think of it as a little token of my appreciation."

"Is she serious?" Lyric rages, kicking the side of my chair as the class cheers.

I fake-smile and say through clenched teeth, "This

is getting out of control. The girl will stop at nothing to bribe Valentine Middle."

Piper passes the cupcake box to Rachel, who's seated at the head of the class. "And to celebrate the midpoint of cookie season, I just want to remind you about the big pool party with pizza and a live DJ—that is, if I win the big Valentine Middle title. It'll all go down at my daddy's hotel, the Parker." She waves her arms and nods at everyone. "And you're all invited."

"Now *that* definitely sounds like a bribe," I yelp before I can catch myself.

Piper gasps, clutching her imaginary pearls like Betty Jean does every time something shocks her socks off. "I'm offended that you would even suggest such a thing. You do know what *incentive* means, don't you?" Piper taps her temple with her index finger. "But, since you mentioned it, if anyone in class wants to rethink their position and rejoin my sales team"—she looks directly at Logan and Dallas—"I wouldn't be opposed to that at all. And being part of my team will get you VIP admission to all the festivities after my big win, so you—"

"The bell is going to ring in a second, Ms. Parker!" Ms. Pepper interrupts.

"Just one more thing," Piper says, holding up the cupcake box. But Lyric doesn't let her finish.

"You already have your dad driving you around town in wrapped food trucks."

"And putting you in commercials!" I spout.

"Students," Ms. Pepper addresses us, with a tone that warns us to chill all the way out.

A group of kids in the hallway poke their heads into Ms. Pepper's classroom. They point to me and wave. One short kid in the front with red sunnies and short braids tosses me a thumbs-up. Lyric nudges my shoulder. "Check your numbers now."

I check my Insta and geek at the latest numbers:

997 views
643 likes

The braided boy sings into the room.

I'm your cookie monster.
No, not an impostor.
I'll keep your cookies comin'.
Sell them by the dozen.

Then the other three boys join him.

Sell them by the dozen.

The rest of the class erupts into a frenzy, and I can feel the burn in my cheeks from smiling so hard.

When I pull up my Virtual App, I see that I've now sold 153 boxes of cookies. The video is doing what it's supposed to do—advertising! And people are actually— *finally*—buying cookies!

"The competition isn't over," Piper says, sauntering back to her seat. "You're really getting ahead of yourself."

"It doesn't look that way to me," Lyric says as the rest of the class sings the chorus, too. Even Ms. Pepper is reluctantly snapping her fingers to the catchy beat.

The bell rings, and my classmates don't waste any time swarming me as Piper, from the back of the classroom, rattles off all the ways they can join her team. The cardboard box is still filled with untouched cupcakes, and I'm overflowing with satisfaction.

EIGHTEEN

When school is over, my scout squad hightails it over to Nicky's Nail Salon and Spa on Montana, next to the Whole Foods and Peet's Coffee. Lyric, Stella Rose, and I are chattering the whole way about the mega events of the day.

"Hi, girls," Ms. Nicky says when we slam through her front door.

We try to keep a standing appointment each month. It's our little way of practicing self-care. Plus the owner, Ms. Nicky, has all the latest colors. She became fast friends with Betty Jean when she got to town a year ago. And it was inevitable; they bonded over everything beauty.

"Hey, Ms. Nicky," I shout, plopping down into the pedicure chair next to the nail bar. I blow her a quick kiss and bend over to roll my boyfriend jeans up to my knees.

Ms. Nicky is the sweetest shop owner in town, next to Betty Jean, of course. She looks to be in her early thirties, but it's really hard to tell because she always wears her hair in two short pigtails with the perfect amount of makeup. She's like that one cool aunt you tell all your deepest secrets to. Betty Jean says we're lucky to have another place to go where we can let our hair down. We never actually take our hair down at Ms. Nicky's—it's all about the nails—but I get what Betty Jean means.

"Good to see you girls today," Ms. Nicky says to Lyric and Stella Rose as they skip through the front door. "Betty Jean texted that you'd be here today, so I arranged to have your faves—fruit smoothies on the house."

"Wow, Ms. Nicky," Stella Rose hoots, checking out the area in the back of the spa that's been sectioned off just for us. "You sure know how to make a girl feel special."

"Well, all my girls are special, but you four are bee-yond," she says, looking around. "But I'm only counting three. Where's little Miss Lucy?"

"Grounded," I say matter-of-factly, and smash my palm into my forehead.

"Her parents finally found out about her shop, huh?"

Ms. Nicky says, shoving her hands into her hips. "I guess her big sister wasn't the best silent partner after all."

"You said it," I sigh as Ms. Nicky turns on the water to fill my pedicure tub. I splash my feet around and kick up a few suds. Then I sit back and exhale, getting comfy in the posh place, like I always do, admiring the shop's view.

Wallpaper with giant green palm tree leaves lines the walls above the marble floors. Every few feet, watermelon-pink pedicure chairs and alabaster nail stations are positioned around the big rectangular room. She even went all out and hung two huge chandeliers at each end of the ceiling. It is downright dreamy. Every shade of color in the universe is stacked on the six-foot nail bar, which seems to stretch for miles.

"Grab your smoothies, girls," Ms. Nicky says as her identical assistant files out of the back room with a tray stocked with three rainbow-colored fruit drinks in tropical cocktail glasses and bendy straws.

Stella Rose plops down in the chair beside me and grabs a drink from the tray. "Let's toast to B and pray that her video goes viral."

"Let me check the Virtual App!" Lyric says, swiping around her phone. "Says here that your sales have doubled since before the video went live."

I check my app, too, and coo when I see that I've sold almost three hundred boxes of cookies today!

Lyric might be onto something. She told me to give it a little time and to trust the process. Admittedly, in homeroom, I was being impatient, but now I'm starting to see the light at the end of the tunnel. It's dim, like a night-light that's meant to keep away the monsters at bedtime, but it's there—and I can definitely see it.

"What palette are you choosing today?" Ms. Nicky asks me as she gently pulls my cuticles out of my mouth. I've been so consumed with my numbers that I didn't even realize I was nibbling on my nails until now.

I point to the denim color next to the peacock blue at the far end of the nail bar and practice my deep breathing. Since my hands are busy, I can't rub my ears or hold my own hand or even give myself a hug. So, I exhale instead. And then I inhale. And I picture myself winning the big cookie crown.

"With our new sales team, there's a chance you just might beat Piper at Friday's cookie tally," Lyric hypes, running her fingernails over the shamrock, sea-foam, and parakeet greens. "And I couldn't be prouder of our girl."

"And there's no way Piper overcomes losing the star players on her sales team," Stella Rose says, showing me her laptop while I wait my turn. "Your YouTube page is blazing hot. And the vid on your IG has over five hundred views. It's been shared a gazillion times."

I pause the pampering and check my Insta, and I'm shocked to see that people are actually liking and commenting. They even left more than a dozen @WeAreGirl-Power mentions.

"Is this even real?" I gawk at the computer screen.

"As real as it gets," Lyric says, taking the laptop from Stella Rose. "And it's only a matter of time before Girl Power notices. Then they'll just *have* to respond!"

"And I'm getting all of this for my documentary," Stella Rose says, now balancing her camera in her arms.

"For your what?!" I low-key freak out, surprised by this new info.

"If you can do it, then maybe I can, too."

I wink at her and smile.

"This is going to be the big comeback *we* need," Stella Rose explains. "Then, in two weeks, the story will be complete. Just think about it. The rise and fall and then the rise again of the Santa Monica cookie queen."

"It does have a glorious ring to it," Lyric says, scooting into the chair on the other side of me with a pistachio-green color in her hand. "I love this one."

Stella Rose grabs a bottle from the bar and holds it

next to her orange-and-black-checkered biker shorts. "I'm in a marmalade kind of mood today."

Lyric holds the pistachio bottle up to the chandelier. Then she announces into the air, "B, let's just call it. You're totally going to win the week three Cookie Countdown!"

I settle into my seat and turn on the back massage as Ms. Nicky cuts my big toenail. I raise my tall, curvy glass in a toast, secretly unsure of how this whole thing is going to pan out. But I don't dare let my girls know.

"To our cookie monster," Lyric says, like one of those announcers at a boxing match. "The soon-to-be-undefeated champion of the Valentine Middle cookie race."

I slurp my smoothie until my head is buzzy.

"Girls, you know what would've gone really good with those smoothies?" Ms. Nicky stops fiddling with my foot and looks at each of us. We're all hanging on her last word, waiting for her to tell us, until...

Then I finally blurt out, "Cookies!"

"Yes, and I'm sure my customers would love some, too."

Lyric nudges me from her chair and scratches at her throat. "Ask her," she whisper-orders.

"Ms. Nicky, would you, uh, be interested in buying some cookies from me?"

"Why, Brooklyn Ace, I'm so glad you asked. As a matter of fact, I would."

"And I bet the car wash would, too," Stella Rose says.

"And the bowling alley would probably go nuts for some. And even the—"

"Businesses! Duh!" I scream, pounding my palm against my forehead. "How did I miss that?"

Lyric wriggles her finger in the air. "And we have a few new heavy hitters on our team who'd be perfect for this assignment."

I shake my head. "We almost overlooked an entire market."

"Don't forget about the barbershops and the furniture stores, too," Ms. Nicky says, smiling proudly at us.

My thoughts race down every block in town. "You know that shop that sells hot tubs on Main Street? The guy who works there always looks hungry."

"But what if Piper Parker already hit up all of these shops?" Stella Rose's eyes narrow.

"But what if she didn't?" I say right back, determined to expand my sales territory.

I sit back and ponder the new strategy. Before I know it, my eyes are closed and I'm daydreaming about all the cookies I'm going to sell. Then my thoughts drift to seeing the look on Piper Parker's face when I pummel her with my new numbers at Friday's tally.

Lyric and Stella Rose slurp down the last of their smoothies. Then we all sigh into bliss.

"That was a rush. I wish I could feel this way every day," Stella Rose says a few minutes later. She looks through the picture window that frames Second Avenue, squirming around in her chair.

"And why can't you feel good every day?" Ms. Nicky asks her, applying the coconut-colored polish to my toes.

"It's just that I finally have a prizeworthy story of B's cookie comeback and it's going to be purrr-fect. But I still have to do my part, and that's where I get stuck. I'm still missing the first piece of the puzzle: my intro. And there's this looming deadline that I have to meet if I'm going to—"

Lyric takes out her phone and shoves it under Stella Rose's nose for her to see. "We can both be brave together."

"What's that?" I ask, fidgeting in my chair, trying to get a glimpse.

Lyric says over her shoulder, "It's personal, so it can't leave this room."

"Ms. Nicky's is a safe space, girls," Ms. Nicky affirms, looking up from my tootsies. "You can always be sure of that."

Lyric whisper-explains, "It's a letter to my mom. I started it, but I can't seem to finish it."

"What does it say?" I ask.

"I started telling her how I feel, you know, that I need her just as much as she needs her career."

"Wow," Stella Rose and I say together, our tongues wagging, waiting to hear more.

"You actually started putting words on the page," Stella Rose says, her eyes saucering.

"Yeah, in Reynolds's class today. B said her therapist insists that releasing your feelings is one of the best ways to wellness. And I know I haven't been taking the best care of my relationship with my mom lately. Our dynamic is actually kind of, well, the opposite of well."

"I'm so proud of you," I gush over my girl. "A month ago, you wouldn't have even considered opening up to us about your feelings, and now you're being all brave and courageous and sharing them with your mom."

"And that's the start of a real letter," Stella Rose says, gawking at the tiny screen. "It's not a text with a bunch of hearts and prayer emojis."

In that moment, I don't think I've ever been prouder of Lyric Darby, not when she won first place performing Beyoncé's "Run the World" at the winter festival or even when she beat out all the boys to play Simba in *The Lion King*—which was downright epic!

"The words will come to you," I say, offering her a bit

of encouragement. I know more than anyone how hard it can be to express yourself when you're hurting. Losing Mom has been the worst thing to ever happen to me, but if I'm being honest, writing to her has helped me declutter my brain so I can start learning how to understand all my jumbled feelings, especially the guilt and confusion.

Lyric glimpses the letter one last time before closing her email. "Brooklyn is my inspo, and I'm putting in the work just like her."

Stella Rose scoots to the edge of her pedicure chair. "So, I guess your point is that I should try to put in the work, too, and record the big intro to my video?"

Lyric presses her phone to her chest. "You got it, sister."

Since my toes are wet, I point to my backpack and Stella Rose hops up from her chair to grab it for me. When she brings it over, I dig around inside until I find what I'm looking for.

"This is for you," I say, handing her the red notebook from Dr. Simone. "It's really helped me out a lot. I just write down my thoughts and my feelings, and it makes me feel lighter somehow."

She takes the notebook and stares at it. "You're giving me your sacred notebook?"

"That's what friends do. And it's really been a lifesaver

for me. Besides, you need it more than I do now. Write down your intro; that should really help, especially since your documentary deadline is around the corner." I take a long sip of my smoothie and grab my forehead from the brain freeze takeover. I squint my eyes and suck in air until it eases. Then I look up at Stella Rose, who is still in shock. "As long as you promise to use it."

She holds out her pinky and I hold up mine. Then we twist them together in the air.

"Write out your script, and if you start to feel nervous or have racing thoughts or feel like a big truck just parked on your chest, go ahead and write all that stuff down, too."

"I never would've thought to do this," she says, gripping the notebook.

"Me neither, to tell you the truth. But I think Dr. Simone gets me." I grin at Lyric. "And she's kind of good at her job, too."

"And so are you," Lyric says, winking at me.

I wriggle my freshly painted coconut toes in the air. "What's my job?"

Lyric opens the email on her phone and continues writing. After a few seconds, she looks up and smiles while Stella Rose nods and says, "Being a really good friend."

NINETEEN

Today was the longest Tuesday in the history of Tuesdays. I'd been waiting all day for the final bell to ring at school. I was geeked because Betty Jean arranged to have the afternoon off so we can hit the Santa Monica streets and score some cookie sales with the local businesses around town. After I emailed a few places yesterday, I heard back from the car wash and the bowling alley. They both said I could come in and present my cookie case. Of course, Betty Jean's assistant gave me a block of time as well. She was the first to respond to my email, which didn't surprise me, as I'm sure Betty Jean had a little something to do with the quick reply. It's nice to have folks in high places.

"Brookie, meet me in the car," Betty Jean says as I slip into my red Converses and check myself out in the mirror. Dad brought my uniform home from the cleaners last night for my big sales day. I hung it on the back of my door instead of in my closet because I hate that fresh-from-the-cleaners chemical smell that all my clothes end up having. I'm willing to look past that today. I grab my sash and bolt out the front door, hoping the stench will air out by the time we get to the big businesspeople in charge.

"Where's the rest of your sales team?" Betty Jean asks as I hop over the side of the door and slide into the white leather seat. I fasten my seat belt as Lyric walks up to the car by herself, holding a piping-hot cup of Starbucks.

"Well. Let's see," I say, counting on my fingers. "Stella Rose has to babysit Ollie and work on her project for the doc competition. And Lucy had to go to an emergency tutoring sesh for math." I open the door for Lyric, and she hops into the back seat.

"Hey, B." Lyric greets us with a quick air-kiss. "Hey, Betty Jean."

"Hi, rock star," Betty Jean says, blowing an air-kiss back at her.

"I was just explaining Lucy's life dilemma to Betty Jean."

"Oh yeah, she's in deep. Her parentals are one step away from sentencing her to a lifetime on punishment!"

I twirl my finger around. "The way they see it, she can't exactly get into med school if she's failing math."

"Sounds harsh," Betty Jean says, pulling out of the driveway.

"It is," Lyric agrees, sipping from her venti cup. "She's got her heart set on going to fashion school in New York City with us, Betty Jean. The plan is for me and B to be at Juilliard together and Stella Rose in film school at NYU and Lucy at FIT for fashion. See, we've got it all figured out."

Betty Jean crinkles her nose and wriggles it from side to side like one of those genies in a bottle. "I'll send some good juju her way."

"Family expectations can be a beast," Lyric gripes, staring into the distance. "But at least her mom is there." I reach into the back seat and touch Lyric's knee, dying to know the status of the letter to her mom. *It can wait*, I think, as I catch her losing herself in her own thoughts.

We ride in silence, letting the fresh air blow through our hair as we approach Pico Boulevard. My long braids flop around and Lyric's blond 'fro dances in the wind.

"You ready for this, B?" Lyric asks, massaging my neck as we approach the first business on the list, BIG BOB'S BOWLING LANES.

"I guess so," I answer. "But how hard can it be? Mom always made it look so easy. Just walk in, flash an adorable smile, and everyone in the place will come running."

"That's not at all how it works, Brookie." Betty Jean glances over at me as she pulls into the bowling alley parking lot. "You know, I've been thinking that it's a good time for Betty Jean's Cookie Boot Camp. We can practice pitching and setting sales goals—plus a few other strategies that could really help pull this whole thing together."

"Boot camp?" I shrug and grimace. "That sounds painful, Betty Jean. And unnecessary. Mom never made me attend boot camp." I put on my sunnies and sit back in my seat. "I got this."

Betty Jean's eyes widen as she grips the steering wheel. "Well, tell me this: What's your big ask? What's your winning sales pitch?"

"My pitch? Why do I need a pitch? It's not rocket science. Mom would always just say a few words and then everyone would gab about how cute they thought it was— how cute they thought *I* was. Then they'd make small talk with Mom for a bit, and before I knew it—voilà!—money was exchanged." I blow a kiss in the air. "I remember it being simple. Straightforward. Easy-peasy."

Betty Jean turns on her blinkers and scowls. It's the look she always wears whenever she's in doubt. "Are you sure you don't want to work on a pitch before we go in? Just a quick dry run?"

I check out my crisp scout uniform and smooth the edges of my hair. I pull down the visor and study myself in the mirror. I was a smash hit last year, and nothing's changed since then. Still the same sun-kissed brown skin. Same chin dimple that winks whenever I chew bubble gum. And still the same round, dark brown eyes with the thick, overlapping lashes. I shrug at Betty Jean. I don't get what the big deal is or why Betty Jean is making this such a thing.

"Well, the way I have it worked out in my head," I say to her, tapping my temple with my fingertip, "my big goal is five thousand boxes. With businesses, I should be able to cover at least three thousand boxes. So far, I have ten businesses lined up, which means I'll need each business to buy at least three hundred boxes."

"Whoa!" Lyric says, swallowing hard. "Do that many people even bowl?"

"I know, I know…it's a lot. But I'm already so far

behind." I shrug. "The good thing is that the manager emailed me saying the bowling alley is having one of its annual tournaments. I'm just hoping they're hungry."

"We talked about setting realistic, quantifiable goals, Brookie. Now, I know you can measure your goal, so it's definitely quantifiable, but do you think three hundred boxes is realistic?"

I plaster a smile across my face and point to it. "It can't be that difficult. See how cute I am?"

"She's definitely cute, Betty Jean," Lyric cosigns.

"It's ambitious, Brookie," Betty Jean says, exhaling deeply. She digs her fingernail into the steering wheel. Then she shifts gears. "But then again, setting high goals can be a motivating part of the sales process. You shoot for the moon, but even if you miss, you'll land among the stars." She parks the car perfectly. "And you, my little Brookie, are a star."

"You can say that again!" Lyric chimes.

"And you would know a thing or two about that," Betty Jean says back to Lyric.

"Thanks, Betty Jean." Lyric blushes. "I do what I can."

I slide out of the car and wring my damp hands down the side of my uniform. Betty Jean and Lyric wait for me as I take a few long, deep breaths.

"You got this, B."

"Thanks, Lyric. Just trying to get my head in the game."

I stare at the big wooden double doors and realize that I'm feeling a little parched. I try to shake it off, telling myself that it's all in my head. When I walk into the bowling alley, I see that the manager was right; the place is packed. I swallow hard when, one by one, the bowlers stop what they're doing and turn to me—and stare. I feel their eyeballs checking me out. So, I do the only thing I can think to do and smile through the bundle of nerves that have set up shop in my belly.

"Seriously, B." Lyric grabs my hand. "You got this. This is your world. Remember, you were made to make sales."

"Now, what should we do next?" Betty Jean quizzes me as she checks out the scene.

I feel my stomach flip around from side to side. "Ask for the manager?" My insides are suddenly queasy, and I feel like I need to vomit, right there in the entryway next to the restrooms. I suck it up and walk up to the hipster in the shoe booth anyway.

"Hey, I'm Beckett," he says, pushing his retro eyeglasses up his nose. An older man with a denim vest nods at us while Beckett changes out a pair of cowboy boots for cool-looking bowling shoes. "I've been expecting you." He hands the hard brown shoes to denim-vest guy and then offers me his full attention. "The manager gave me a heads-up that you'd be stopping by. You think you might want to make your big announcement over the speaker?"

"My announcement?" My mouth has become abnormally dry. I smack my lips a few times to help, but there's no use: I'm now *completely* parched. I look around for water. *Where's the water?!*

"Yeah. Aren't you the Valentine Middle scout selling those cookies?"

Everything is happening so fast. "Duh. Uh—yeah. Of course I am," I stammer, trying to sound prepared and in control. But I'm not—not at all. I didn't expect to present to the entire bowling alley filled with strangers who are solely focused on knocking down vulnerable pins with heavyweight balls. An older woman who could play a grandma in one of those hearing aid commercials crashes her bowling ball into a triangle of pins. She gets a strike and wickedly screams, "Gotcha, suckas!"

"You picked a good day," Beckett says, completely unaware that the grandma is over there trying to knock the pins unconscious. "There's a waiting list for the lanes. This Santa Monica Seniors Tournament is one of the biggest tourneys of the year."

I stare at the menacing grandma. "Uh-huh."

And before I can utter another word, Beckett turns on the speaker and walks out of the booth with a microphone.

He bends down to hand it to me and walks away. "It's all yours," he says over his shoulder as he sidles up to the concession stand.

I fumble with the microphone, causing it to make a loud screeching sound. *That can't be good*, I think as everyone cuffs their ears and turns around to find the source of the annoyance. And yep, it's me. All *me*!

"Just pitch your little heart out, Brookie," Betty Jean encourages me.

My eyes shift to Lyric, who is watching me fumble the ball *big*-time. "Are you having those same feelings you did back in the gym at cookie cookoff?"

I nod, scanning the room.

Everyone is watching.

Lyric doesn't experience any degree of stage fright when she's onstage. In fact, she morphs into a whole other person, singing to the heavens, shaking her Hollywood hair so it blows in the imaginary fan. I'm the opposite of that person right now. Nevertheless, Lyric does her best to encourage me anyway.

"You got this. Just picture them in their undies," she says, shrugging, unaware that Mom would've told me to do the exact same thing.

"Hi, uh, hi." The mic flips and flops around in my hand until I'm finally able to fumble through a few more words. "I'm, uh, Brooklyn Ace. And I'm a seventh grader at Valentine Middle School." My voice cracks and I sound like a toad falling off a lumpy log. "I'm, uh, here today selling...uh—uh—uh—"

"Cookies!" Lyric yelps, nudging my belly, hitting me somewhere around my large intestine.

"Right. World Scouts cookies."

"Cookie queen," Lyric says as Betty Jean shakes her head and clears her throat. "Tell 'em you're the reigning cookie queen!"

"Yes, I was," I say, bobbing my head up and down, not repeating the most necessary part of the pitch at all.

"What's your goal, Brookie?" Betty Jean whispers to me.

I give up when my thoughts escape me and the bowlers go back to, well, bowling.

"I'm, uh, working to be the top seller in all of America—I mean, Santa Monica, this year."

Beckett shrugs when the last few people who were paying attention completely lose interest. And I know this episode of the cookie chronicles is over when the mean grandma turns to me and snarls. It's at that exact moment that I start to feel dizzy and the walls get ready to swallow me. *I know what to do*, I think as I dig into my tool belt and try on a few strategies.

I reach for my ears and press into them.

Then I press harder.

But nothing happens.

I try clutching my sweaty hands together and pressing into them while I count down from five.

"Five, four, three-two-one—five, four, three-two-one." I shut my eyes and motor through the numbers a lot faster than Dr. Simone demonstrated. But when I don't feel any relief, I throw in the towel and race back to the front door, trying to outrun my embarrassment. I can feel Lyric on my heels as I bolt out of Big Bob's Bowling Lanes as fast as I can.

This definitely isn't going to be as easy as I thought.

I hear Betty Jean's words sizzle through the air behind me. "Let me know when you're ready for Betty Jean's Cookie Boot Camp, Brookie."

I roll my eyes, fighting back the overwhelming feelings of defeat, and run faster toward the car.

TWENTY

It's my least favorite day of the week again: FRIDAY!

I can't even believe I'm saying this, but the love/hate relationship I'm in with Fridays is starting to feel really wicked. And I'm not the only one having all these negative feels.

Stella Rose zips up her backpack and slings it over her shoulder. "I made the rounds with Lyric to Beach City Car Wash yesterday to represent Brookie's Cookies," she starts explaining, swatting at the air when her bag gets tangled in her scarf. "And let's just say, Piper Parker's sales team didn't miss a single beat."

"They're still everywhere, and I mean *every*where!" I

exclaim as we head out of Mr. Reynolds's English class. "Even without Logan and Dallas!"

"I hit up two barbershops and a nail salon on my way home," Lucy says. "Before I could get in the door, they were ushering me back out. Piper's crew had already been there taking orders an entire twenty-four hours before me."

"Well, that can't be good," I say, slogging up to my locker. "Do we really need to go check the Friday cookie tally this week?"

Lucy taps her foot against the floor. "Yes! Pootie's going to read the results, and we missed him doing it the last two weeks."

"And?" I sulk deeper.

"Annnd...I want to hear him announce that you're the queen bee this week."

I snortle at her and belt out a loud, "*Humph!*"

"B," Lyric adds, "you never know how this is all going to unfold. You have to show up for all of it. And soon enough, you'll get more businesses to invest in your brand. It's only a matter of time." She fluffs her big spiral curls. "We just have to be diligent and work the system."

"If you say so." I trudge down the hall toward the tally board outside Principal Pootie's office.

"Can I have your attention, students," Principal Pootie says, addressing some of the kids hanging around the bulletin board. A few boys bounce basketballs in the hallway, causing him to scratch his throat and fuss. "Please, stop that right now!"

He gives them a stern look, but they don't stop until their coach blows a whistle loud enough to make everyone jump a few feet into the air.

"Thanks, Coach," Pootie says before turning to the tally board. I glance at it, still unable to focus on the list of names scribbled there. All I see are the cutout letters:

VALENTINE MIDDLE
WORLD SCOUTS COOKIE SALES
WEEK 3 RANKINGS

"Since you've gathered at the cookie tally board, I'll take this time to read off the rankings."

He scratches his butt and some of the kids snicker. But he just ignores them and says, "Don't forget about the band competition starting this weekend as well as the basketball tournament, where our Valentine Bees will be playing in the second round."

A kid with wavy red hair geeks, "What about the science fair happening in the lab, too?"

"Yes, I was just about to say that." Pootie waves his hand around his head.

Lucy folds her arms over her shaggy knit jacket and snides, "Can he just say the rankings already?"

"Or slide over so we can read them ourselves," Lyric agrees.

"Try to relax, B," Stella Rose says when I push my fingers into my mouth and gnaw on my cuticles before I realize I barely have any left.

"I just want to know!" I whine. "How badly did she beat me?"

"This week, students," Principal Pootie says, adjusting his reading glasses and getting right down to it, "not much has changed since last week. Piper Parker is still in the lead with one thousand boxes of cookies sold."

Stella Rose tightens her yellow-and-blue cashmere scarf. "She's a cookie crook."

"A total crookie!" Lucy whisper-sulks.

"Crud!" I squeal, and stomp my foot into the floor. Principal Pootie stops and balks at me.

"And, Ms. Ace, you are this week's big comeback kid. That was quite a music video you released," he says, doing the now infamous "Cookie Monster" dance. "You've managed to climb all the way from fifth at the first-week tally to a sweet second-place ranking with nine hundred and seventy-five boxes sold—above Margaret Miller."

Principal Pootie wipes the sweat from his forehead.

He reaches out to someone in the crowd and says, "Congratulations, Ms. Parker! That's a whole lot of cookies! We've never seen this kind of cookie story unfold at the midpoint of the race...well, not in the history of Valentine Middle. Even Valentine High is impressed."

The small crowd hoots and hollers, but all I can focus on is Piper Parker when she steps in front of everyone and takes an actual bow.

"Take your bow, too," Lyric hypes over the crowd, pushing me forward. "You're right behind her! You're the official cookie monster!"

"Yeah," Lucy says, shoving her fist into the air. "You moved up a whole spot and now you're on her butt."

"Ew!" Stella Rose squeals.

A group of seventh graders pushes past me in the small crowd.

"I can't wait for the pool party," one kid with a face covered in freckles says to a boy hobbling past us in a leg cast. "You think your calf will be good by then?"

"It better be," he quips back. "I've been selling cases of those dumb cookies for Piper so I can go to the pool party and jump off the diving board."

"She's totally going to win, bro; half the school is on her sales team. There's no way that other girl will ever catch up to her now."

I turn to my squad and point to my chest. "Me, I'm *that other girl*," I whine as the assistant principal, who looks like Little Red Riding Hood, dashes out of Pootie's office and shuffles up to him, whispering into his ear. We all stand silently, watching Pootie's eyes pop and his head cock to the side.

"I think he's staring at me," I whisper-gasp to my girls.

"No, it's an optical illusion," Stella Rose says. "It just looks like that because there are so many kids in his line of vision."

"Uh, no, it's not an illusion," I correct her when he motions with his index finger for me and Piper Parker to follow him.

"Girls, in my office, please," he says as he shoos the rest of the Valentine kids away.

At a snail's pace, I follow Piper into Pootie's cluttered office. I sit down in the closest armchair next to the door and cross my legs at my ankles. If there's anything I hate more than spiders, it's being called into the principal's office. It makes me feel like I'm about to get scolded, or even worse, suspended from school. Then I start to think about what Betty Jean would do. Would she be so disappointed in me that she'd leave me and Dad alone to fend for ourselves in this big world? We couldn't make it without her—there's just no way. So I absolutely can't get in trouble.

"Girls, we have a situation," he starts.

I do my best not to look at Piper, who has her hands folded on her lap and a tight, fake smile plastered across her face. She looks like a model student, but I know better. Despite my best attempts at ignoring her, I glance in her direction when she sneezes. On autopilot, I say, "Bless you."

She shoots me a death glare that slowly settles into a smile. "Thanks."

"You're welcome," I say back, again on autopilot.

Crud!

I can't let my guard down around her; she's a mean-girl monster and I'm her prey.

"We seem to be caught in quite a bit of red tape," Pootie says as Piper turns back to him and bats her lashes.

"What could you possibly mean, sir? We've been running a fair race."

"Not according to the Cookie Council," he corrects her as I scoot to the edge of my seat. "It appears that you both have violated rule twenty-six B from section four."

"What the heck is that?" I yelp, tossing my arms into the air.

"Does this have something to do with her music video?" Piper asks in a very accusatory tone that I'm really not feeling.

"Well, what about your big television commercial that didn't have anything to do with cookies, but with your daddy's hotel?!" I fight back without flinching.

"Actually, girls, it has to do with both!" Principal Pootie says, rapping his fingers on his desk. He takes out his kerchief and swipes it back and forth across his forehead. But the tiny beads of sweat just pop back up. "The Cookie Council says you're both in violation and that you're breaking the rules with the commercial *and* the music video."

"But we worked hard on that video! We had to come up with a song and then lyrics and then a whole thing with where we were gonna shoot and then—"

"I get it, Brooklyn, but this is above my pay grade." He looks at the document in his hand and sighs. "You should be very proud of what you accomplished, but the Council has decided that all advertising needs to go through official scout channels only."

"What does that even mean? I can't make a video?"

"You can, but the rules are very specific about how that needs to look moving forward. I'll be emailing you both the updated mandate." He takes a deep breath. "Look, I'm pretty sure the Council just wants to keep the playing field fair for everyone."

I stomp my foot onto the floor. "But that's just it. I

had to make a music video. How else am I supposed to compete when she keeps taking all my Old Faithfuls and beating me to the businesses?" I point at Piper and yell, "I'd be willing to bet that she's got spies everywhere giving her intel on me and even—"

"You wish," Piper says. "I'm outperforming you because I'm a better sales queen."

"No! You're a cheater," I quip back.

"Girls! Girls! Stop this right now," Pootie says, lowering the baritone in his voice so we know he means business. "You're both incredible and very creative in your approach to selling cookies, but now we need to remove all the bells and whistles and get back to good, old-fashioned sales strategies that have been approved by the..." He looks down at the document and says, "World Scouts Alliance Cookie Council."

"But what about all the sales I generated already from the commercial?" Piper asks.

"And my music video?!" I huff.

"That's the good news. The Council is going to let you keep them. But moving forward, no more advertising that doesn't happen through approved channels."

I chew on my fingernails and slouch back into my chair. "Jeesh, Principal Pootie, that's way harsh."

"But at least all our hard work will still be counted," Piper says, slouching in her chair just a little.

"Yeah, that's true," I say, shocked that she's the one in the room who found the silver lining.

"I just hope my dad will see it that way, too," she mumbles.

"What's that mean? You're killing this game. Why wouldn't he be on board with finishing fair and square?"

"Don't worry about it. It's really none of your business," she says, and folds her arms over her chest.

I shrug and turn back to Pootie.

"But I see your point," she finally says. "It's just not that straightforward for me."

"You've been in first place since this thing started. I just don't get what you have to worry about. And your dad should be super proud of you. Right?"

Begrudgingly, I hold out my hand to her and wait for her to shake it. But when she doesn't, I finally say, "Okay, Pootie—I mean, Principal Pootie. You're right; we can do this without all the bells and whistles. We're both creative and talented—no matter what anyone says."

I look over at her, and she half smiles.

I try holding out my hand to her again, but this time I'm starting to feel like a jerk because she clearly has no intention of shaking it. Mom always told me to take the high road and be the best version of myself. So here I am...trying. And after a few extra-long seconds, to my surprise, she shakes it.

"Great!" Principal Pootie says, and pounds his fists onto his desk. "This is great. Now, there's a list of acceptable sales channels in your scout handbook, and it says here..." He runs his finger down the document. "It says here that if you have any questions, your troop leaders can call the Cookie Council directly."

I stand, ready to bolt from his office, but before I can, Piper Parker stops me.

"Brooklyn, can I say something?"

"Uh...to me?" I look at the door and wince when I realize I was centimeters from dashing through it. "What's up?"

"I, uh..." She turns to Pootie and twists her neck around until he takes the cue to give us some privacy.

"Don't mind me," he says. "I'll just be responding to the Council's email."

"I just want to say that I know you think I'm savage or whatever you and your friends call me."

"How did you know—"

"But I'm not."

I shove my hands into my pants. "Then why do you act like you are?"

"It's complicated. But since you asked about my dad, and no one ever asks me about stuff, I just wanna say one thing."

"First, Piper, I asked because it matters. All of it matters. And that includes you."

I watch Piper take a few long, deep breaths, and she appears to be…nervous. I've never seen her this way before, and I'm dumbfounded. Yes, dumbfounded! But I lean in and listen just in case she has something to share.

"You might not know this about me," she says, avoiding eye contact, "but being a winner is the only thing that matters to my dad. It's the only time he sees me—when I win. So, I have to win at everything, even selling World Scouts cookies."

"I—I didn't know that."

She grabs her white leather backpack and looks at me without blinking. Then she says, "There's a lot you don't know about me."

In that moment, I realize that she's right. All we knew was that she transferred here a few weeks ago from who knows where and jumped into the cookie race with all her might. Maybe, just maybe, I was wrong about Piper Parker. Maybe she does know how to spell N-I-C-E.

"Listen, Piper, there are a lot of ways to compete, and all I'm saying is that you don't have to be so cutthroat about it."

She leans in closer and doesn't blink. And with her whole heart, she says, "Sometimes I do." Then, without looking back, she walks straight out of Pootie's office.

TWENTY-ONE

After school, Magic and I are sitting in Dr. Simone's waiting room, and let's just say that after Pootie's big announcement about the Cookie Council's decision, I'm not feeling optimistic about my chances of becoming the next Santa Monica District queen.

"You seem...oh, I don't know..." Magic taps her chin, studying my face. "Sad today."

I grip my cell. "You can really read me, huh?"

"That's what happens when you're friends."

Magic places her hand on my shoulder and leans closer. "I bet this has something to do with what Principal Pootie said about our music video." She shows me something on her phone and peps, "You're still a winner—everyone at school is doing the 'Cookie Monster' dance. I still can't believe it!"

"I don't mean to downplay all the hard work you guys put into making the video go viral, but it stinks that those sales won't matter moving forward. I was really counting on them to push me over the top." I take her phone and put it on the table next to the magazines. "Now I have no earthly idea how I'm going to win."

"But now you and Piper are on a level playing field," she says, picking up her phone and putting it in her pocket. "You're both at roughly a thousand sales and every move you make going forward will be about sheer will. And you've got more heart than she'll ever have. You're made of atria and ventricles, and all the other cool stuff we learned in science class."

"Facts," I say, nodding.

"And Piper is made of black goo and smelly residue."

I can't help but giggle, but then I admit, "She's not so bad."

I scroll through my phone and check out the video again, sharing the screen with Magic. "I am proud of what we did. That sick Michael Jackson moonwalk move you came up with is my fave part of the choreo."

Magic and I mark the "Cookie Monster" routine,

getting hyped. She likes the part where we all hold hands and fall into the splits. She gets up to show me that part, only she struggles to hit her split. That just makes us laugh harder until a notification drops onto the screen. It's a text from Lyric: **911!**

"What's wrong?" Magic asks, hopping back into her seat.

I shrug and open Lyric's urgent text: **Piper's Insta. Brace yourself!**

My fingers start to tremble as I pull up my ex-nemesis's IG. And then, right there, is the nail in my cookie coffin: a *regram* on Piper's feed from…GIRL POWER!

> **Grab your cookies from our fave World**
> **Scout, Piper Parker. Link in bio.**

"What?!" I screech, losing all feeling in my fingers.

"Is that real? That can't be real." Magic's face crinkles around her frown. "Can it?"

My palm is too sweaty to hold the phone. "That clearly violates the rules. Pootie said so. I'm pretty sure the World Scouts Council didn't approve rock stars advertising for us." The phone slips between my fingers and tumbles onto the hardwood floor.

"Maybe regrams are okay?" Magic stares at my phone,

barely blinking. "Or maybe because...maybe it's okay because Piper didn't do it, but someone else did? Maybe?"

I suck my teeth and growl.

"I'm just throwing spaghetti at the wall over here, trying to make it make sense."

"You can come in now, Brooklyn," Dr. Simone says from the door that leads into her office. I'm falling down this emotional rabbit hole so fast that I don't even hear her walk in until Magic nudges me.

"Oh, hi," I say, out of breath. Then I turn to Magic, who seems to have lost all color in her face, too. When she waves at Dr. Simone, it looks like she's seen a ghost.

I try to stand, but all the feeling in my feet is gone. And I still can't catch my breath. Then the room starts to feel smaller, and the walls loom over me as I shrink into a bundle of nerves. But this time I don't surrender to it: Instead, I take off my sneakers and my ankle socks and crawl to the wall behind me. I stand up and press all my body weight against it, focusing on one thing in the room, the magazine stand in the corner, as I count backward from five—four—three...

Dr. Simone and Magic watch me, never uttering a word, as I do the anxiety exercise again. I make sure to count even slower. "Four...three...two...one..."

"I'm okay," I announce to the room. "I am."

"Good job," Dr. Simone says when I gather myself enough to grab my socks and shoes and pad into her office, my head still in a haze.

Listlessly, I plop down on the edge of the couch, my crossed ankles rocking back and forth.

"That was pretty groovy," Dr. Simone says, taking a seat in the chair in front of me. "You've mastered that exercise since I saw you last." She applauds me without making too much of a stir.

"Grabbing my ears or massaging my hand didn't really work for me the last time," I say to her.

"You have to do what's best for *you*. That was some pretty awesome self-care I saw back there."

"I've had a lot of time to practice," I admit. "So much stuff is happening, and it never seems to let up."

"So, everything isn't okay, I take it."

"No!" I yelp. "Not okay at all."

"What's going on?" she asks, reaching for a tissue box.

"I'm not going to cry. Not over Piper Parker," I declare. "But…but…" And then a tear falls anyway.

Stupid tear.

"It just isn't fair."

Dr. Simone hands me a tissue, and I blow my nose—hard!

"Do you want to tell me what happened?"

"Every time I take one step forward, it seems like she runs three zillion circles around me." I grab a few more tissues from the cardboard box.

Dr. Simone straightens her onyx-and-sapphire bow tie and leans closer. "Something to do with Piper Parker, I assume."

"You're assuming correctly," I say, and pass Dr. Simone my phone, which is still open to Piper's page.

"Oh." Dr. Simone blinks hard—and then harder. "Wow." And faster. "Really. That's…wow."

"I know, huh!"

"Isn't Girl Power *your* favorite band?"

I start ripping the tissues into tiny pieces. "They're, like, *everything* to my entire squad."

She picks up her clipboard and scribbles down a few words. "I see."

"How does Piper Parker even *know* them?" Before I know it, I'm sobbing into the tissue, but mostly onto my clammy hands.

"Brooklyn," she says, crossing one leg over the other to reveal matching onyx-and-sapphire socks. "I know this must really feel like a disappointment for you."

"The Cookie Council says they won't count sales from my music video anymore, and those were going to put me

242

over the top. Our video went viral and I was going to win. I was going to *win*!"

She folds her arms over her crisp sky-blue shirt. "And that's something I want to talk to you about in today's session."

"I mean, finally. It was happening. I came in second this week, and I was inching closer to snatching that first-place ranking from her." My eyes shift around the room, stopping on the sad taupe curtains. "My music video, it was the freshest thing Valentine Middle has seen."

"I'm sure it was if you had anything to do with it."

I blow my nose so loud my tonsils tremble.

"Brooklyn, can I ask you a question?"

"Uh-huh," I sulk.

"Why are you doing this? Why are you selling World Scouts cookies? What's in it for you?"

"What kind of question is that?"

Duh. To win.

Then I think about it.

Carefully.

I want to tell her that I'm doing all of this to help kids around the world who need schools, that I'm doing this so I can make the world a better place. But something inside won't let me. So I don't tell her anything.

"Well? What do you think?" she presses.

I sniffle into the striped sleeve on my fleece hoodie. "I get it."

"What do you get, exactly? Let's talk about it."

I slide down into the velvety couch cushions and suddenly feel really small.

"Do you think that maybe you've lost track of why you were doing this in the first place?" she asks gently.

I rip the one small thread from my sleeve cuff that's been dangling around my wrist. Then another thread pops apart from the rest. I can't bring myself to look at Dr. Simone and face the truth, so I switch gears and fuss with the cuffs on my eggnog-colored denim shorts.

"You've been focused solely on winning."

My glassy eyeballs finally make contact with hers. I hold back another tear, determined not to fall apart like that one thread that was holding it all together.

"What do you think your mom would say?" she asks in that same warm tone that makes me want to be honest with her—and with myself.

"Maybe that I lost track of everything, you know, the important stuff." I reach for another tissue. "And maybe she'd say that she's disappointed."

Dr. Simone slides her clipboard onto her desk and folds her hands in her lap over her distressed jeans. "I don't think there's anything to be disappointed about after you realize that you've just gotten a bit off track."

"I think I might've turned into a real live cookie monster."

"But at least you caught yourself. Sometimes it takes adults most of their lives to get back on track. And you're twelve—a brave twelve—but twelve, nonetheless."

"Believe it or not, I really do want to help build schools for kids around the world. And even make their lives better, you know. I have all these awesome opportunities, Dr. Simone. And to share some of my gifts was what this thing meant to me from the start."

"I know," she says, scooting to the edge of her seat.

"So. Where do we go from here? I'm not really sure what to do now. Without Mom here it's all a big blur. With Piper getting an endorsement from Girl Power, I'm clearly going to lose the race. And I guess I've lost perspective on this whole thing, too."

"But...did you?" She leans in with a smile.

I look up at Dr. Simone and take a long, deep breath. We don't say anything to each other for about five whole minutes. Then I glance at the door, and the words topple out of my mouth. "I keep waiting for her to walk through. But she never does."

"That's the hardest part to accept sometimes. It's not

easy, all the memories and leftover feelings that we have when we lose someone we love." She waits a few seconds before she says what I really need to hear. "What you're going through... it's okay, perfectly okay, to miss her and long for her just the way you do." Dr. Simone rests her palms on her knees.

"Can I be honest with you?"

"Always."

"Sometimes I feel like I got cheated."

"Most people would agree that Piper Parker hasn't played fair."

I shake my head. "No." I blink a few times and then announce, "You're right; she shouldn't be my focus anymore."

"Well then, congratulations, Brooklyn. That's what we call real growth. Clarity. An epiphany."

"What I'm trying to say is that I still wish I didn't have to do this life thing without Mom."

Dr. Simone gets up and sits beside me. She doesn't say anything until I look at her and sigh.

"I completely understand how you feel. It hurts to not have the person you've always looked to for love and support and encouragement."

That's when I start to ugly-cry, bawling big tears, like the weight of the world is running over my cheekbones. For the first time, I feel like I've let my mom down.

Somewhere in this race to be the best, I lost track of why I was even competing. I wanted to win so badly that it all became about beating Piper Parker at her game, and I forgot that I was playing my own game—one that Mom put so much love and compassion into that was all about being of service to others. She would never have lost sight of the big goal—to help those in need. If she were here, this never would've happened.

Dr. Simone gets up and hands me a pen and her clipboard.

"Let's go back to what works for you," she says, attaching a fresh piece of paper on top of her notes. "Use your written words to express your feelings."

I take it from her and stare at it for a few moments before jotting down some things. Then I show it to Dr. Simone, who reads it aloud.

> Dear Mom,
> Nothing about you being gone feels fair. I never imagined doing this life thing without you. But you will forever be a part of me, and that means that I'm like you—pretty strong. It also means that I can get it right. I promise to finish the race and be the champion you would want me to be. I'm sorry for forgetting.

"I do know one thing for sure," Dr. Simone says after reading my wet words.

I look up at her for an answer.

"She'd be very proud of you today. I know I am."

"I realized something, too."

"Realizations are what help us move forward. Would you like to share?"

I close my eyes and just blurt out my truth. "I really depended on her to do a lot of stuff that I didn't know how to do."

"Like what?" she asks softly.

"Like pitching to my customers. Betty Jean says I have to learn how to tell people I don't know who I am and what I'm doing and why I'm doing it. But I get so...so...anxious and scared that I turn into a hot mess and my words get all jumbled and my body feels like it's not my own."

"I see. Those are some heavy feelings."

"I know, right? See, that's why I needed the music video so much. I didn't have to say anything. The song and the fresh dance moves said it all for me."

"Have you considered that you can still learn how to do all those things on your own?"

"Betty Jean says she can teach me. I've been putting it off, mainly because stepping up to the plate and using my own voice is terrifying—without Mom."

Then the more I think about it, the more tears join my pity party. And I cry until I don't feel like crying anymore.

"Betty Jean says that success is when preparation meets opportunity." I exhale into a thought and ease myself from the couch. "There's something I need to do."

"Do you maybe want to talk about it? Share it with me?"

I wipe my damp cheek. "I promise to tell you all about it next week when I see you."

"Next week it is," Dr. Simone says, standing, too. "And, Brooklyn..."

I turn around when I reach the door. "Yes?"

"Congratulations on a big win today. You now have everything you need inside of you already." She walks me to the door and says, "You truly are a champion."

TWENTY-TWO

The next day, I shoot Betty Jean a text to remind her to meet the scout squad (minus Lucy, who's still grounded) at the farmers market for Cookie Boot Camp.

> **The girls are all here and we're ready for you. Can't wait to get started. Meet us outside the Foot Locker on Arizona.**

Stella Rose, Lyric, and I head down the next three blocks and around a corner, and walk straight onto Arizona Avenue, where the farmers market is in full swing, which is no surprise since it's a gorgeous Saturday by the ocean. There are tons of people out today picking up their fruit and veggie haul. I always loved coming here with Mom every weekend; she'd make a beeline for the honey stand on Third right away.

"Guys! Wait up!" I hear a familiar voice in the distance, and we all turn around just in time to see Lucy running toward us.

"What are you doing here?" I geek, padding over to her and shrugging. "We thought you were on punishment for life."

"I would've been," she says as she digs into her backpack, and pulls out a brand-new iPhone.

"They finally caved!" Lyric gasps.

Lucy scrolls to Fashionably Ranked, a tween website where kids list their fave online boutiques. My mouth drops when I see her name, right there, in bold pink-and-gold letters. She's ranked in the "Accessories" category. I press my fingers on the screen and enlarge the words:

#4 Mini Mogul to Watch:
LUCIANA LOPEZ

"That's you!" I screech. "You're...famous!"

"Not quite, but it was enough for my parents to finally take me seriously. After my sister showed them all the money I was raking in and a bank statement from my savings account, let's just say they came around."

"Whoa," Stella Rose says, holding up her phone. "Your horoscope says you're on the road to redemption today."

"Fun fact: My folks said if I'm going to really do this thing, I have to pay taxes."

"It always leads back to math," Lyric explains, shaking her head. "I bet you won't miss another tutoring sesh now."

"I'm scheduled for three days a week," she says, laughing. Then she gets serious. "My one regret is that I didn't bring all of me and my passion to them sooner." The sides of her mouth twist into a pout. Then she nods for emphasis. "There's something to be said about facing fears head-on."

"Proud of you," I tell her, admiring her courage.

"Thanks," she says, just as Stella Rose loosens her tie-dyed infinity scarf and points to the Gap store.

"It's Betty Jean!" Stella Rose yells.

Betty Jean beams at each of us as we take turns smothering her in hugs and high fives. On the way to the Energy Bee Farm's stand, she listens to the latest revelation at my Piper Parker pity party.

"Can you believe that, Betty Jean? She got Girl Power to endorse her!" I pout, as she nods and picks up a jar of bee pollen. Then she smiles. I know she's thinking about Mom; I always do whenever it involves honey or bees or pollen or basically anything that has to do with that species. "What is it that I always tell you, Brookie? Never underestimate—"

"The competition in business," I finish.

"Yes! You have to always stay ahead of them at all times." She walks past a few tables before stopping in front of one marked MURRAY'S FAMILY FARMS.

Lucy pops a few grapes into her mouth. "Can we just fight back with a celebrity endorsement of our own? Or with bribery like Piper Parker was trying to do with the whole seventh grade before Logan and Dallas ditched her when they finally saw her true colors?" She pops a few more green grapes into her mouth and chomps down on them. "Are you going to teach us that in boot camp?"

"Not if you want to win fair and square," Betty Jean says. "And you can, with the right campaign."

"Yes, the right campaign," Stella Rose parrots Betty Jean. Then she says, "What kind of campaign, exactly?"

"We'll cover all of that in my boot camp," Betty Jean says. "We're going to focus on three things, girls: the product, the marketing, and the sales."

"I know everything about the cookies," I say to Betty Jean, skipping ahead to the table with the cucumbers, tomatoes, and olive oil. I pick up three ripe tomatoes and try to juggle them. "I know the different flavors, *even* the vegan and gluten-free ones." When I almost drop a tomato, I place them back in their bin and mouth *Sorry* to the girl behind the table, who looks like a fairy in her glitter wings. All she's missing is a bedazzled leotard and a smile, because the scowl she's giving me isn't very fairylike.

"That'll come in handy," Betty Jean explains to me. She grabs my hand like she used to do when I was a little girl at Disneyland.

"I didn't know we offered vegan cookies," Stella Rose says, her eyebrows dancing a jig. "I can sell to my cousin and my aunt now. They both went vegan for the new year."

"Two new customers!" Betty Jean high-fives Stella Rose. "Brookie, what about nutritional info? Which cookies have the most calories? Or the most fat or sugar or protein?"

I shake my head and shrug. "Now, *that* I don't know."

"If you have a prospective customer who's concerned about having too much sugar, then that information would come in handy, right?" She eyes me and smiles. "There's one important thing that I have to circle back around and address."

I cringe because I know exactly where she's going.

"You have to have your pitch down, too, Brookie." Even though I blew the big opportunity at the bowling alley, she never made me feel bad about it, didn't even say "I told you so" one single time.

"Uh-huh," I mumble, deciding not to admit to her that face-to-face sales just isn't my thing—not with my belly full of nerves. It's like Beyoncé. She never really does interviews; it's just not *her* thing. But she still sells a gazillion records with sky-high downloads from streaming. Yeah, that's me: the Beyoncé of cookies.

Betty Jean wriggles her finger at me. "If you want to beat Piper Parker at the cookie game, this is just the beginning." She blows us all kisses and walks away toward the table with the almond pastries, nut butter, and a big, flappy sign that says FAT UNCLE.

Once I realize how much work I have to do, I suggest moving class to my house, where I can focus on the business at hand and not be distracted by blueberry muffins and homemade jam.

Twenty minutes later, we rush down the hallways, into my bedroom, frenetic energy whizzing around us.

Stella Rose shoves my dirty clothes aside and sits on the edge of my bed while Lyric kicks off her loafers and slides into the hanging chair. "Now can we talk about campaigns? I want B to have a killer one. But first, what is it? Is it anything like running for class president or for treasurer?"

"That's a totally different type of campaign," Lyric explains. "Betty Jean means like all the back-to-school ads we see everywhere. Think corporate. You know, businesses."

"Like when McDonald's rolls out the McRib sandwich every year. They have all the commercials and billboards," Lucy says into a sigh. "Now I want a McRib."

"That's a good example, Lucy." Betty Jean looks around the room for a place to sit. She decides to slide into my oversized beanbag by the picture window. "A campaign is when a company promotes its product or service with an advertisement." We all watch as she sits crisscross apple-sauce before leaning in closer to us. "And you're right—it can be on television with commercials and on billboards, but also online, on the radio, in magazines—"

"I can't afford anything that cool; besides, the Council put their foot down and isn't allowing anything to be sold outside approved sales channels."

"We'll just have to think of something even bigger," Stella Rose says, winking at me.

"And better," Lyric cosigns.

"Lyric?" Stella Rose whisper-asks. "Do you think you could reach out to your mom again and maybe a few of her influencer friends? We can tag them and even ask for a designated post."

Lyric sighs, never answering Stella Rose, who pulls up Lyric's mom on Insta.

"She already did," I explain.

"But I'm on her IG now, and nothing about B and the cookie competition is posted," Stella Rose says, then gasps. "Holy macaroni! She has two million followers."

Lyric tries to hide her disappointment. "It's whatever."

I never like putting her in an uncomfy position, especially when it makes her feel bad about her relationship with her mom. So I move the convo along. "I totally get it. And it's cool."

"Sorry if I brought you down. I was just thinking that since your mom is so famous and we're, like, totally not..." Stella Rose's voice trails off.

"And Piper is *clearly* using her resources," Lucy finishes.

"We'll be just fine," I say to my scout squad, and pad over to Lyric. I take her hand and say, "All of us."

"I know you girls are looking for something out of this world to help launch Brookie's Cookies into the stratosphere, but there's an opportunity to learn a valuable lesson here," Betty Jean says, looking us each square in the eye. "Sometimes it isn't about bigger. Sometimes it's about good, old-fashioned connecting. You've done it already, the door-to-door sales, the big phone-a-thon. That's real-life connecting to people, and it can be your most powerful tool. Sometimes, believe it or not, you don't need all the bells and whistles."

"So, no more businesses?" I ask, tapping my chin.

"I didn't say that," Betty Jean laughs. "I think expanding your sales territory to include businesses was a brilliant strategy. But one critical thing has been missing."

Stella Rose shrugs in confusion. "But when Lyric and I went, they basically slammed the door in my face. What did we do wrong? Was it because they'd already bought from Piper?"

"Actually, I don't think it had anything to do with Piper," I say, starting to make sense of it all. "I think I should be the one to hit them up. That way, they can form a real live connection with me, the scout behind the Brookie's Cookies brand."

"Now you're getting it," Betty Jean says.

"So basically, I need to go back to the barbershop and the car wash and the..." My voice trails off when I think of the big double doors.

"Yep, B, and the bowling alley, too."

I feel my insides start to curl into a big ball and tighten

at the thought of stepping back into Big Bob's and pitching at the lanes.

"No matter what, I'm really proud of you girls. You've grown so much already, and you've put in the hard work. Your infrastructure for all your online sales is already set up beautifully. And all your socials are driving traffic back to Brookie's Virtual Cookie app, and you even came up with a few creative hashtags to build a community for her customers and fans." Betty Jean is almost in tears when she says, "And the name of the brand, Brookie's Cookies, just warms my heart."

"We did everything we could think to do," Lucy says.

"But I know something's missing," I say.

For the next fifteen minutes, we sit in my bedroom and lose ourselves in thought. Stella Rose massages the back of her neck while Lyric crinkles her forehead. Lucy pokes the eraser on her pencil into her forearm, and I take a bunch of deep sighs every few seconds.

"Okay, my creative brain is fried," Lucy finally says. "I'm all tapped out."

"I know what's missing," I say sheepishly. "I've known for a few minutes now."

All eyes are on me as I stand up and announce, "I don't have a strong pitch."

"That's my girl," Betty Jean says, clutching her signature single-strand pearls.

"Thanks, Betty Jean and Lyric, for not dishing to the whole room about my Big Bob's wipeout. It's no secret that pitching has been my kryptonite."

"We all have one," Stella Rose says.

"And despite the fact that I'm getting bubble guts at the thought of venturing back out into the world to talk to strangers again without Mom, who's been my secret sauce for my whole cookie career, I think...I'm finally ready."

And just like that, I am.

TWENTY-THREE

It's the final week of sales and time for me to get down to business. Literally.

After school on Monday, I go straight home and focus on one thing: my pitch!

I scribble the last few words on the paper in front of me. Then I stand up, facing my diverse audience of teddy bears, and take a deep breath.

Betty Jean says eye contact is critical, so I look each and every one of them right in their plastic retinas…and then I go for it, standing up straight and trying out my memorization skills.

"Hi, my name is Brooklyn Ace and I'm a seventh grader

at Valentine Middle School. Last year I was crowned...I was crowned...I was—

"Ugh!" I fret when I keep getting stuck in the same place. I eye my teddies but luckily they can't say anything. I toss my sash over my tie-dyed tee, take a deep breath, and try again.

"Hi, my name is Brooklyn Ace and I'm a seventh grader at—"

"At Valentine Middle, baby!" Lyric sings into my room. To say that I'm embarrassed is an understatement.

I rush to toss a stack of clothes over my stuffed animal audience and turn around to find Stella Rose right behind her.

"I was, uh, just, uh..."

"You were practicing like a pro," Lyric says, bounding into my bedroom. "Don't worry," she mutters between slurps of her Starbucks. "I use my framed photos of close friends as my audience. I line them up in rows on the table and practice all my new songs."

"Well, now I don't feel so silly," I admit.

"You shouldn't," Lucy says, sashaying into the room. "I practice my catwalk up and down my hallway at home. I have to be ready for my first big fashion show when they shout out the designer and I have to make my celebratory walk down the runway. I'm still trying to figure out if I'm going to take a bow or do a series of twirls." Lucy is in deep thought when she says, "Or maybe I'll just toss up the peace sign like Stella Rose does every time she takes a picture."

Stella Rose giggles and flicks her the peace sign. Then she turns to me and says, "Your turn. Show us what you got."

"Yeah, B," Lucy says. "We can be your audience. Dazzle us."

"Okay, but first let me look over my script one last time," I say, grabbing the crinkled piece of notebook paper where my pitch is scribbled. I check the scene and rattle off my pitch with nervous enthusiasm, making sure to slow down when I reach the end. "...and I'd love your support toward my mission, and so would the Grief Center, where I'll be donating a percentage of the money raised from my sales."

I hear one sniffle and then another and then a loud horn-honking sound, and I immediately know it's Betty Jean blowing her nose behind me. She pads over to me and throws her arm over my shoulder. "It's just so...touching."

"Yeah, especially the part about the donations," Dad says over Betty Jean's shoulder.

Stella Rose forms a heart with her hands and puts it over her chest. "I just love that you're doing that."

"We're hashtag proud of you, B, for drafting an incredible pitch," Lyric says while the other members of my scout squad make little hearts with their hands and place them over their chests, too. "Big Bob's Bowling Lanes isn't going to know what hit 'em."

I had decided to go back to the scene of the crime first, and that meant staring Big Bob's Bowling Lanes and all my angst about it straight in the face, before hitting up the other businesses on my list. It was better to get the big monster out of the way and just...slay! I'd been working on my pitch and practicing my timing, so I didn't have as much stinkin' thinkin' to deal with that would throw me off my square. Now all I had to do was show up and show out.

Betty Jean sniffles one last time and then gets back to business. "They're right; that's an excellent pitch, Brookie. And in your follow-up, don't forget to tell them all about the product."

"Got that covered," I say, pushing my shoulders back into my spine. "I'm ready for the vegans, the gluten-free customers, and even those watching their figure."

"That's good, 'cause my peeps are always on a diet," Lyric says.

Stella Rose stops putting her camera away to snap her

fingers. "You're a total pro now. You probably know more about those cookies than the bakers."

"Speaking of bakers," Lucy says, batting her lashes.

"Let me guess...some of my famous apple pie today?" Betty Jean's smile covers her whole face.

Walking over to Betty Jean with her arms wide open, Lucy wipes away fake tears. "Bring it in, Betty Jean. Right here." Lucy hugs Betty Jean tightly. "You get me."

After we scarf down more than a few bites of apple pie à la mode, Betty Jean drives us back to Big Bob's Bowling Lanes. I hop out of the car and march right up to the big double doors.

It's now or never.

"That's our girl!" Lyric yelps into the air as my scout squad follows close behind.

I open the enormous heavy metal doors, take a deep breath, and walk inside.

"Hey, Scout Girl," Beckett says when he notices me standing in front of the weathered wooden desk.

"Hey, Beckett," I say, never breaking eye contact. "Good to see you again. And thanks for taking my call."

"You were serious about that do-over, huh? I didn't really expect to see you again after...well, you know."

"Sometimes in life, Beckett, it's not about the final destination; it's about all the things you learn on the journey getting there."

"I see," he says, and hands me the microphone exactly like the last time I was here. "The floor's all yours, kid."

I look around, smiling and greeting all the preoccupied bowlers with my eyes. They seem to either be clueless, or they couldn't care less about why I'm here. But I'm determined to not let it stop me. This time is different; I'm finally ready to step up and use my voice to advocate for what I want. Not having Mom here as part of our dynamic duo was a big blow to my heart, yes, and my sales, too, quite frankly. But I've learned one thing for sure: I already have everything I need inside me; Mom made sure of that.

I watch one guy cup his ears when the microphone makes a series of screeching sounds. *I better hustle*, I think, not wasting any time doing what I should've done the first time: *my very best!*

"Hi, everyone." I feel my fingers drawn to the seam on my sash. "Um, good afternoon." I pull my hand back and place it by my side. "My name is Brooklyn Ace and I'm a seventh grader at Valentine Middle School. Last year I was crowned the school's cookie queen, and this year I'm working to meet my goal of selling five thousand boxes of cookies." I flash a confident smile as one by one, the folks in their striped bowling shirts from lanes two, four, and seven stop and turn around. "I'd really appreciate your support for my mission and so would the Grief Center, where I'll be donating a percentage of all my sales."

There. I'm doing it. Almost done.

When I feel myself start to fidget with my sash again, I grab the microphone with both hands. "The scout who sells the most cookies in Santa Monica will qualify for a trip to London to work with the World Scouts Alliance to build schools around the world. I'd like to be one of those scouts. I know that with your help, we can make the world a better place."

And...I'm done. I actually did it. I made it to the end.

Most of the bowlers are now watching me watch them. I hand the microphone back to Beckett, who says, "Not bad, kid."

"Thank you." I exhale into a nervous smile. I extend my hand, gripping his firmly, when he bends down to shake. "I sincerely appreciate the opportunity."

"You know what?" he says, standing up straight and digging into his pocket. "I'll take a few boxes."

"Really?" I pep. "That would be great."

A woman in lane two with long side bangs and a yellow-and-black bowling shirt that says SPARE CHANGE throws her hands into the air and yells, "Me too."

"Can I get some as well?" asks a lady who looks like Ms. Pepper, my homeroom teacher.

I blink a few times in a double take and say, "Sure! Of course!"

I glance at Betty Jean and my scout crew, and I can't help but swell with emotion. The most overwhelming feeling I'm having is pride—and hope. That's when Lyric shows me her phone, and I watch her press SEND on her big email to her mom. I wink back at her and decide that hope is definitely winning today.

I'm interrupted only when the guy behind the concession stand waves his hands around his belly and barks, "Save some cookies for me."

"And me too," the husky kid in overalls next to him yells.

And just like that, over the next two hours, I go from lane to lane, pitching my heart out, until I sell almost three hundred boxes of cookies. And this time, it feels right. And fair. And no, it isn't Mom's voice out there convincing everyone to buy cookies from me. It is mine.

And it is good enough.

TWENTY-FOUR

I wake up on the final day of cookie sales still groggy from a night filled with tossing and turning. I had dreams of zoo animals dancing through the Santa Monica streets, singing our "Cookie Monster" theme song. They were wailing the words, stopping only to eat Pinkberry mango froyo.

"Good morning, Brookie." Betty Jean brings me a glass of freshly squeezed orange juice. "How's my champion feeling today?"

"Well..." I start, not totally sure myself. On one hand, I'm excited to see how my numbers have stacked up to Piper's. I spent every day after school this past week selling my heart out to the barbershop and car wash customers. I even made more trips back to Big Bob's after Beckett sent me an email that said I had to come back because Tuesday was Ladies' Night and Wednesday was Eighties Night. Then I couldn't miss yesterday because it was Movie Night and they were playing *Grease*, and everybody was dressed as their fave character. Between all the businesses, especially good ol' Bob's, I managed to sell a stellar 2,677 boxes of cookies. I barely got any sleep and got called out in Mr. Chang's class because I was snoring, but almost hitting my goal was well worth it.

"You should be over the moon after you proved to yourself that you're talented and capable of doing something that you weren't so sure you could do."

"I am very proud of myself, Betty Jean."

"That's good because we're all proud of you, too." Betty Jean pulls the comforter back and scoots closer to me. She moves my braid away from my earlobe and makes sure I hear her when she says, "When you started this thing, you were afraid of talking to people you didn't know, you were scared of putting yourself out there."

"That's because Mom wasn't here to help me."

"But you used everything you've learned from her and put it all into being the best version of yourself—and she's a big part of that."

"Do you think she'll be proud of me, even if I don't win?"

"Remember what we said," Betty Jean reminds me. "It's not about winning today at the rally."

"I'd really like a shot at building schools for all the kids who could use my help."

"I know, Brookie, and that attitude and perspective are exactly what makes you a winner already."

I check my phone and sigh, turning it around so Betty Jean can see the latest and greatest. "That's a lot of likes," she says, cocking her head to the side, studying Piper Parker's Girl Power regram. "Eleven thousand!"

"And counting." I fidget with the frayed edge of the comforter.

Betty Jean reaches for the picture of Mom and me that I had in bed next to me and stares at it. "No matter what happens today, remember her and how you've strengthened your bond. That'll help get you past whatever emotions come up today." Betty Jean pinches my cheek. "She was a lot like you, ya know."

"She was?" I roll over onto my elbows.

"Well, when she had her mind set on something, there was no talking her out of it. Just like someone else I know around here."

"You mean Dad?"

"No, silly, not Dad."

I grab my ears and pull on them. "I'm all ears. I haven't heard any stories about her in a while...." My voice trails off when I try to picture her smile. Then I quietly admit, "Sometimes I worry that I'm going to forget her."

"That'll never happen," she says, shooing me with her fingertips. "Now. What would you like to know?"

"For starters," I say, glancing at my phone, "how did she handle disappointment?"

"You'd be surprised. That was one thing she didn't handle too well—at least not at first. But over time, she learned that giving it her all and doing her best were the only things that really mattered."

I turn the phone over so I can't see the screen. "The same lesson I'm learning now, huh?"

"We all have to learn that lesson at some point. No one is born ready to take on the world." Betty Jean crosses her legs and grips the picture frame as she starts telling me a story. "I remember she told me about a time when she was running for class treasurer. Just like you, she was always top in her class and really good in math, so it should've been a no-brainer. But there was a boy—"

I pull the pillow over my face again. "*Why* is there always a boy?"

"Well, this particular boy—let's just say your mom

had the biggest crush on him—until he ran against her in the election."

"Oh no. That sounds like a disaster waiting to happen."

"I'd say. And then when he beat her by only a few votes, she was crushed."

I toss the pillow to the floor and sit up. "What did she do?"

"She married him."

"No way," I say, giggling and falling back onto the bed.

"Total way," Dad says, walking into the room. "And I never regretted beating her in that election."

"That's one of the best stories I've heard in forever." I look at them both and clarify, "But, for the record, I have no intentions of marrying Piper Parker."

Dad laughs, easing past all my clutter in the room to sit on my bed beside Betty Jean. "Can I say something that I think you might need to hear, especially today?"

"Shoot. I'm listening." I watch him fidget with my comforter like he's carrying the weight of my world on his shoulders. He reaches for my hand and squeezes it.

"I want you to know something, kiddo." He takes a deep breath and touches my cheek with the back of his other hand. "You're all kinds of incredible. And I don't know if I could've gotten through this if it weren't for your strength."

"Dad..." I say when my heart starts to beat super fast.

"Just hear me out." He looks at me with the warmest eyes and says, "If you don't know anything else, always know that you're my number one reason. And I'm so proud to call you my daughter."

"Wow. But I didn't do any—"

"You found the courage to do it all, and even when it got really hard, you kept going. And that's why I've kept going, even on those days when I didn't know how I could go on without seeing your mom's sweet face." He takes a deep breath before continuing. "I miss her every second of every day. But I watch how determined you are to get through this, and it inspires me."

I squeeze his hand back. And I listen, holding on to every word he says.

"We're in this life thing together, Brooklyn Aerial Ace, and I'm proud to be on your team."

"Thanks, Dad, so much," I say, getting choked up at his raw sincerity. Honestly, he's not usually this open with the emotional stuff. And because of that, I try to remember everything he's just said so I can replay it again later. "I love you."

"I love you more, kiddo," he says, patting Betty Jean's knee and then heading for the door.

"He's a proud man, Brookie, and he adores his baby

girl," Betty Jean says, picking up my phone. "And it looks like he's not the only one." She points it at me. "I think you need to check out some of these comments in your Virtual Cookie app. Do you, by chance, know anyone in London?"

I shake my head. "Nope."

"Because this person from London says she loves your passion and that, I quote, 'I hope your cookie dreams come true—yours truly, from London.'"

"Someone wrote me all the way from London?" I gasp.

"And she bought a bunch of cookies, too." Betty Jean scrolls through the list of comments.

"But how do they know about me? The music video was making waves, but when the Cookie Council stepped in, Piper had to stop running her commercial and I had to take the video down."

"I don't know how you're a superstar, but look," she says, pointing to another comment. "You certainly are. There's another one here from Tokyo. It says 'Ganbatte kudasai,' and the one under it is in Spanish, Brookie: 'Buena suerte.'"

"O-M-Cookie-G!"

"And the next one is in French." Betty Jean starts fanning herself. "And then there's even one from Russia.

"This is incredible." Betty Jean wipes away the tear that's forming. "I don't know how, but you're the cookie flavor of the month, and now all these people from around the world are buying cookies to support you and wishing you luck."

"I've gotten almost five hundred new orders since last night." I shake my head in disbelief. "We went all the way global!"

Later that day at lunch, I hightail it to my locker, where my scout squad is waiting. I shove my phone into their faces. "Did you guys see this?!" I'm jumping up and down and their heads are bobbing with me, until Lyric finally grabs my wrist to get a steady look at why I'm so hyped.

"This is amazy!" she yells over my hoots and hollers.

"Can you believe this? I have no idea how any of it happened."

"I have a confession," Lyric says, blushing. "I may know who kick-started all the viral madness." I watch Lyric as she smothers a series of giggles. "You'll never guess."

"I think I might actually have an idea," I confess, looking at all the regrams of a post from late last night. "Your mom…"

"She sure did!" Lyric gushes, showing me her mom's Instagram page, where she shouted out my scout squad and posted a series of pics of us as babies wearing only our diapers and a slobbery smile. Then she told all her followers to check out the "coolest kids in the cookie biz!"

"We're famous!" Lucy says. "I never thought it would happen this way, but... we're famous!"

"And that post is within the Cookie Council's sales rules, just like Piper Parker's regram."

"I can't believe it," Stella Rose says, pointing to herself on the far end of the pic. "Jade Darby even mentioned the Grief Center." Stella Rose grabs my shoulder. "This is huge, B!"

I spin around and pop my scout collar. "Jade Darby called us the coolest kids in the cookie biz!"

"That's my mom! And those are her words." Lyric puckers, pressing the phone to her lips.

"Ew!" Lucy spouts, pushing the phone away from Lyric's pucker. "But yes! Way cool."

I'm out of breath when I ask her, "How did this happen?"

"She said she read my email and that she'd do anything to make it up to me. Also her words," Lyric swoons. "I'm still in shock. And I wish she was here to explain it to you herself, but I'll take it." Lyric stares lovingly at her mom's Insta. "I'm proud of her for this."

I open my locker, still in shock. "I owe her farealz!"

"No, you don't. She might've also said that her

manager thought it'd be a good look for her brand, too."
Lyric shrugs. "Hey, I'll take what I can get."

Lucy folds her arms over her chest and cracks a smile.
"We think you should check the cookie app again. But
how about you do it on *my* phone?"

Lyric, Stella Rose, and I giggle at Lucy.

"So does your parents' big turnaround mean you don't
have to go to med school?"

"Ha!" She leans against the locker beside mine and
shrugs. "I'll let you know when they get off that train. But
as of right now, I'm enrolled in a pre-med summer program in San Diego."

"Baby steps," Lyric says. "Look at how long it took for
my mom to notice me. First you get the kids, then you
get—"

"The moms!" we all yell in unison, still giggling.

Lucy passes me her phone, which already has the
cookie app open, while Lyric hovers over my shoulder, all
of us staring at the screen in disbelief. "Says here that your
last order came from Perth."

Stella Rose's eyes study the ceiling like she's searching
for an answer.

Lucy cocks her head to the side and sighs. "Australia.
Duh!"

I pat Stella Rose on the back. "I wouldn't have known either except one of Betty Jean's favorite dating shows is filmed there."

"And the orders are still coming in." Lyric scans the cookie app and grins. "This is all from Jade Darby. I bet Piper Parker didn't get seven hundred new orders overnight from all over the globe."

Stella Rose scrolls through the comments. "And sweet greetings from World Scouts around the planet!"

"Humph." I ponder that for a second. "But I bet she *already* had seven hundred, or more like seven thousand, from Girl Power posting about her!"

"These numbers say you're still in this thing," Lucy advises. "I'm not giving up just yet."

"I don't know, guys. She's a real contender. And she's been ahead of me this whole time. I learned my lesson, and I'm not underestimating my competition ever again."

Stella Rose checks her watch. "You have thirty minutes before the final cookie tally."

"So...what's the plan?" Lyric asks, tapping her chunky heels against the floor.

That's when I spy Piper Parker at the other end of the hallway. She's peeking around her locker, watching me, flanked by Rachel and Lindsay. My squad watches her squad right back. And when I close my locker, Piper closes hers, too. Then we just wait...until I grab my phone and motor to Mr. Chang's classroom.

And within seconds, Piper Parker and her crew are on our heels.

"Let's try to lock down orders from the teachers," I yell over my shoulder. "At this point, every sale counts."

"I couldn't agree more," Lucy says, checking her spreadsheet. "You have almost a total of forty-five hundred boxes sold, and most of them came from pitching to the businesses in person."

"I have to sell as many as I can...in thirty minutes," I huff, rounding the corner into Mr. Chang's classroom.

Stella Rose checks her watch. "Make that twenty-six minutes."

"Mr. Chang!" I yell as he erases the mixed fractions on the whiteboard.

"Mr. Chang!" Piper yells at him, too, as she barrels into the classroom.

"Yes, girls, what's up?" he asks, turning around to see us both shoving our phones into his face.

On autopilot, I delve straight into my pitch. "I'm Brooklyn Ace...and I'm a seventh grader at Valentine Middle. I'm selling World Scouts cookies—"

"He knows who you are, duh!" Piper scoffs at me,

before turning back to him and smiling politely. "Would you be interested in buying scout cookies this year?"

"Yes, Mr. Chang," I say, recovering. "From *me*?"

"*No!* From me," Piper says.

"I asked him first!" I say.

"But I started my pitch first!" she says.

"No! You didn't."

"Well, I meant to."

I roll my eyes at her, suck my teeth, and ease toward his desk, tossing my backpack onto it. When I unzip it, I pull out four boxes of cookies, one of each flavor. "I have samples, Mr. Chang. And for you, a very special customer, I could leave you with them. That is, if you'd be willing to buy from me."

"That's not fair!" Lindsay barks.

"Why not?" Lyric and Lucy fuss back together.

"Samples equal good marketing," Stella Rose says. Then she turns back to us and whispers, "Clearly she didn't go to Betty Jean's Boot Camp."

"Girls! I'll buy from both of you. How's that sound?"

I nudge Lucy, nodding at the order form. Before I can catch my breath, she steps forward, getting my drift, and takes his order while I speed out of the classroom and head around the corner in search of more grown-ups.

On my way down the hall, I stop to secure orders from the janitor, the school nurse, and the cafeteria lady.

Out of the corner of my eye, I spy Piper hitting up the basketball coach and the office manager. We are locked in a stare-down when I hear my homeroom teacher. And you guessed it: She's next on my hit list.

"Ms. Pepper! Ms. Pepper!" I yell into her classroom before checking over my shoulder to see if Piper is on my tail. And this time she isn't.

"Yes, Brooklyn, how can I help you?"

I'm out of breath, but I pitch to her anyway. "Hi. My name is Brooklyn Ace and I'm a—" I stop when I realize I'm doing it again. "You already know who I am. Listen." I fan myself. "Would you like to buy cookies from me?"

"I already bought cookies from you...at the first rally of the season. In the gymnasium."

That's right. She sure did. In my madness to get all teachers on my order form, I completely forgot.

"Oh yeah. I'm sorry about that," I say, and fly out of her classroom.

"But I'll buy another box," she says before I hit the hallway.

Stella Rose, Lyric, and Lucy bound into the room, and I nod at them to finish the order.

"Thank you, Ms. Pepper. You have no idea how much I appreciate that."

"Sure thing. I have to say that I was impressed with

the fact that you're donating to the Grief Center. That place does a great job of helping so many kids who have lost loved ones. You make me proud, Brooklyn."

As she finishes, I'm reminded of my reason why I started this whole cookie takeover in the first place: to help people. Dad said I was his inspiration earlier, and now I guess, if I'm being honest, Mom is that very special inspo for me.

Before I can get choked up, I eye Stella Rose, who mouths back to me that I have fourteen minutes left before the bell rings and the cookie race ends.

"That's so wonderful, Ms. Pepper. My scout squad will finish you up. And again, I appreciate the opportunity...and that means that I appreciate *you*!"

Lyric points down the hall, dabbing her forehead with an imaginary kerchief. Immediately, I know she means Principal Pootie. I toss her a thumbs-up and dash out of the room.

I speed past clusters of kids and empty classrooms, poking my head into each one, in search of a teacher—any teacher. At this point, I'm basically just looking for anyone with a wallet or a bank account.

"Principal Pootie!" I gasp for air when I see him locking up his office. And then I see her.

"Too late," Piper says. "I got to him first."

I slip in front of her and plead with Pootie. "But, but..."

"I'm sorry, Ms. Ace, but I make it a habit to only buy from the first scout who asks. That way I keep my funds and my waistline in check." He pats his belly, then grabs his kerchief from his back pocket to dab at his forehead. "And this year it was Ms. Parker." He walks toward the stairs that lead down to the gymnasium. "I was wondering what took you so long to come get my order, Ms. Ace. You were first in line last year. Or wait—was that your mother?"

"It was my mom," I say sullenly.

Lyric whistles at me from down the hall and points to a classroom.

"But I'll get you next year," I say, and bolt toward Lyric, Stella Rose, and Lucy.

As I race down the hall, Piper and her girls are right beside me, heading for what looks like the very last adult in sight.

"Mr. Reynolds!" I call out to him before I can even see him.

"Yes?" he says into the air, his voice floating around my braids as I bounce into his room. Piper Parker tumbles in right behind me, but this time we don't waste words; instead, we both shove our phones under his nose.

And then the first bell rings!

"I'm sorry, girls," he says. "My orders have already been taken by Margaret Miller."

"Please, Mr. Reynolds, just one box of cookies from me," Piper begs him.

"Well..." He checks the clock on the wall above the SIMILES AND METAPHORS sign. "I have five minutes. Let me hear the best of what you have."

"Okay," I say, shoving my nails into my mouth, feeling the pressure of the moment. "I'm, uh..." I take a deep breath and force my hand behind my back. "I'm donating a percentage of my sales to—"

"The Grief Center," he finishes. "Yes, I heard. Very noble of you, Brooklyn." He looks over at Piper. "And you? What's the best part of your pitch?"

"Um...well, um...we didn't really *have* to donate to anyone. It wasn't a requirement."

"Yes, I know, Piper. That's what makes it noble."

"Well..." she says, scrambling, "I'm sure I could get my dad to offer up a weekend getaway to a cookie customer chosen at random." She blinks her lashes and plasters on a smile. "And you never know, it could be you."

"She's good," Lucy whisper-gasps into my ear.

"In that case," Mr. Reynolds says, "I'll buy ten boxes of Chocolate Marvels from you, Brooklyn." He cuts off the lights in the classroom while Lucy follows behind him to take his order. "Well done, kiddo. I'm sure the kids at the Grief Center could use a little help. They need it more than I need a weekend getaway."

Lucy high-fives Lyric, who fist-bumps Stella Rose, who squeezes me into a hug, while Piper Parker and her crew spin on their heels and slither down the hall just as the second bell rings.

TWENTY-FIVE

We march into the gymnasium, comparing notes on all the sales we managed to get in the last twenty-nine minutes.

"I can't believe Principal Pootie didn't budge," Lucy says.

"He was right, though. Through this thing, I've learned a few valuable lessons, and one of them is to step up and use my voice to ask for what I want. And now I know I can do it."

Lyric flashes a zillion-dollar smile at me just as the reporter moseys up to us with his camera in his hand.

"Hey, Brooklyn, how about a shot of you at the podium?

Right next to the grand prize?" He points to the tickets to Disneyland and the shiny new bicycle on the big bee at center court. "Would be cool to have it for your big win over Piper."

I can feel the smirk on my face tighten when I say, "Let's just wait and see how things pan out."

"But you're the cookie comeback kid," he says, reading from his notes. "If the number of eyes watching your music video was any indication, then you're definitely the winner." He shoves the camera in my face anyway. "This article practically writes itself."

"Well, the comeback kid says that we're going to wait and see, so we're all about that patient life over here," Lucy says, putting her hand in front of his lens and waving him off.

I check out some of the HoneyBees who are already on the court stretching.

"Looks like it's go time," I say as Lyric tugs on my cheer uniform and fluffs my rainbow braids, which have been parted into two big ponytails.

"Knock 'em dead," she says, still holding my sash. "I'll have this waiting when it's your turn to switch back into your champion cookie scout uni."

Stella Rose gushes, "You're totally like Supergirl with all your superhero costumes."

I pose and say, "Saving the world one toe touch and box of Chocolate Marvels at a time."

"Break a leg," Stella Rose says, getting her camera ready to record the HoneyBee routine. "I think this'll be my opening shot. Then I'll work my way backward through the story for the doc."

I bend down to tighten the shoestrings on my sneakers. "I'll make sure to give you lots of HoneyBee face." I stand and flash jazz hands into the air.

I take my place beside a few of the other HoneyBees on the court as Magic and LuLu skip over to me, leaving a few of their new adoring fans in the bleachers.

"Did you see that?" Magic hugs me and points at Mr. Reynolds, who's under the basket doing some of the "Cookie Monster" dance moves with the sixth graders. "We've been getting tons of requests to do TikTok dance videos and to be—"

"In the school musical, too!" Winnie finishes, rolling up to us and finding her place in formation. "They asked if we'd be the lead dancers in *The Wiz*. They said we'd make perfect munchkins."

"Now, that sounds like fun," I admit. "That should be our next adventure."

The principal interrupts us with his usual sputtering into the microphone. "Everyone, can I have your attention? Let's get ready to start the rally with our very own Valentine Middle HoneyBees!"

LuLu spins around and checks out all the kids who are eye-stalking us. The way they're staring is different today, and the gym is so quiet you can literally hear a pom-pom drop. "Guess what routine we're doing today," she announces to me.

"No way!" I yelp, just as the intro to "Cookie Monster" begins. And the crowd goes wild!

"Yeppers!" Magic yells, hitting her starting pose. "LuLu taught the rest of the HoneyBees the routine before school this morning."

Magic starts the choreography and I rush to catch up. She motions for me to join, and the rest of the Stumbles pump their fists into the air. Dancing to our song in front of everyone and seeing the whole school hitting the choreo with us is so wild!

There's only one person who isn't enjoying this moment in time. That's right—Piper Parker. She's standing with Lindsay and Rachel, and her arms are folded over her chest. I smother a snortle when Lindsay breaks out into the routine and Piper nearly has a conniption. Between body rolls, I watch her stomp her feet and wave her arms over her head in front of Lindsay's nose like an octopus. I feel bad for Lindsay, but that girl really needs to find her voice and stand up for herself.

"Wow!" Principal Pootie says from the podium as we grapevine through the last of the cool choreography and end with our hip-hop poses. "Looks like I have a new dance to learn."

The HoneyBees skip off the court and take their spots in the bleachers while Principal Pootie gets his notes together. The crowd stomps their feet on the bleachers, and we high-five each other.

"This is a big day for some of our students," Principal Pootie says. "It's the end of a very exciting cookie season and an even bigger day for Valentine Middle. It looks like the Santa Monica District will be crowning one of our very own as the cookie queen this year."

The crowd cheers, and several of the kids sitting around me muss my hair and shake my shoulders. I glance down the court on the other side of the gymnasium and see the kids around Piper Parker doing the exact same thing. *Ugh!* It looks like it's down to her or me, and although I made peace with not being the winner yesterday and then again this morning, right now I'm feeling alllll the feels.

"Before we announce our big winner, I want to

acknowledge the Valentine Middle varsity basketball team. They brought us a big W this week against Lincoln, and now we're on our way to securing that title against Roosevelt. As for our other title today..."

I check my phone to see the latest Virtual Cookie report:

BROOKLYN ACE: 4,835 boxes

"I'm almost at my goal of five thousand."

Stella Rose pans the camera around to me and mouths, *I told you.*

"Honestly, I think you have this in the bag, B," Lyric says. "Your numbers are rising by the hundreds! Whoa!"

"Yeah," Lucy cosigns, snapping a pic with her phone. "I've checked and rechecked these numbers, and the crown should be yours, girlfriend."

Principal Pootie shifts in his loafers. "We are proud of all our scouts who participated in the cookie challenge. All of you are winners," he says, reaching for his kerchief. "This year our top five sold more cookies than any season at Valentine Middle. Rounding out the top five, selling seven hundred four boxes of cookies, is Margaret Miller. Let's give her a round of applause." The crowd claps for her as Pootie loosens his tie. "Fourth place goes to...Rita Argyle," Pootie says, waving his arms in the air when the energy starts to die. "Let's give her a few big congratulatory claps as well. She sold seven hundred thirty-two boxes of cookies this season."

I check the app again.

BROOKLYN ACE: 4,938 boxes

Even though I'm almost at my personal goal, I still have no idea how many boxes of cookies Piper sold.

Pootie waves for Ivory Sandberg to approach the podium with the other two girls. "And our third-place winner, selling almost two thousand boxes of cookies, is Ivory Sandberg."

Ivory stands beside Margaret and Rita, and takes an awkward bow. The kids stop clapping before Pootie says, "I'm sure you all have figured out our top two cookie girls: Piper Parker and Brooklyn Ace."

Piper Parker is already on her feet, waving to her fans, approaching the podium. It's like she thinks she already owns the crown. I sigh, shoving my entire nail bed into my mouth.

"This is it," I say through cuticle nibbles as I stand up.

"This is the moment of truth." Slowly, I trudge to the podium and take my spot next to my biggest competitor.

Principal Pootie leans down and says to us. "You girls should be very happy with what you've accomplished. But there can only be one winner."

I shove my shoulders back, my heart skipping a few beats.

The whole school waits while Principal Pootie swipes at the beads of sweat that have formed on his head. Then he finally rattles the paper in his hand. "It is with great excitement that I declare Piper Parker the Valentine Middle cookie queen *and* the Santa Monica District queen this year, too. Congratulations, Piper. You've certainly made us all proud."

And that's how it ends.

Well…almost.

When Piper slinks up to the podium, I slide in between her and the microphone before she can.

"Can I just say one quick thing first, Principal Pootie?"

He looks back and forth between me and Piper, and then shrugs. "Go ahead, Ms. Ace."

"Thanks," I say, and tug on the mic until it's in front of my face. "I just need a minute."

The crowd watches me, waiting for me to say something. But then I don't.

Awkward.

I realize that I've just lost, and yet, I'm standing in front of the whole school.

What was I thinking?

The crowd fidgets, squirming in their seats. Waiting. *Exactly* like four weeks ago.

Okay, so now we're probably way past awkward.

Some of those same irritating, public-speaking butterflies flit around the pit of my stomach again. *Ugh.*

Principal Pootie makes that gross hacking sound with his throat. *Double ugh.*

The image of the student body in their Fruit of the Looms makes me smile, and I can't help but think of Mom. And then I clasp my hands together and count from five...four...three...two...

"Hi, uh, everyone," I start, flitting my tongue around my mouth. Yep, teeth are still all there. "I just want to say thank you for making this such an exciting cookie season. And although I didn't win, I know that I couldn't have sold almost five thousand boxes of World Scouts cookies if it weren't for the encouragement I've gotten from each of you—even you," I say, turning to Piper Parker. "Most of you don't know this, but I lost my mom to cancer a year ago. And this season has been really hard without her. I've learned a few things going through this race without her by my side. And I thought maybe some of that stuff could help you, too."

I press my hands together tightly—silently counting again.

And I don't forget to breathe.

"I've learned that stuff can get tough, and, well, that's okay. We all have our challenges in this whole life thing. And that's okay, too. I've been fighting with the stupid walls trying to swallow me up lately, but that's a whole different story for another day."

I wipe my forehead and see Stella Rose pan her camera around to capture the attentive crowd. Then she turns the focus back to me.

"But no matter what we're going through, I just want to say that we're enough . . . just the way we are. We're good enough, smart enough, talented enough, strong enough."

I watch Stella Rose look from behind the lens, and then I wink at her.

"We're brave enough."

She grins, taking it all in.

"I miss my mom. And I still hate cancer. But I know that my friends and family have my back, and I wouldn't trade that for anything—not even the grand prize."

My scout squad yells out, "Gooo, Brooklyn!"

Magic, Winnie, and LuLu pip and squeak, too.

Piper tries again, this time with more force, to scoot the mic from my lips.

"And if I can say one more thing." I grab it back from her and rush to get my words out, but then I slow down when I hear the "Cookie Monster" music start to play in the background.

I turn to Piper and say, "Thank you for pushing me to find my voice. Now I know for sure that I'm strong enough to do it—all of it—on my own, even with that mean grandma lady snarling at me in lane two at Big Bob's."

"I don't know what that means," she says, shifting in her heels. "But...cool."

I extend my hand to her, and she just looks at it for a few seconds. I'm not sure if she thought it was going to bite her or burn her, but she takes her sweet time before reaching out to shake it.

Then the unexpected happens.

"You ran a really good race," she says. "And you actually helped me set higher goals than I would've if you hadn't been challenging me." Even Principal Pootie looks shocked. "So, I guess what I'm trying to say is, thank you for helping me be my best."

"You know, you did that same for me," I admit. "And, Piper..." I decide to move the microphone away from my mouth when I say, "I'm sure your dad will be proud."

"You didn't have to say that, but thank you…and yeah, I hope so." Then she just stands there, staring at me for a few uncomfortable seconds, before she spins around to whisper something to Pootie.

He crinkles his brows and checks with her. "Are you sure?" He looks back at the prizes before nodding. "Okay."

I can't take the weird tension any longer so I step back and say, "Welp, that's it for me." I turn to step down from the podium when he stops me.

"Brooklyn, it appears that Piper isn't too keen on going to London after all."

"I've been, like, a thousand times, soooo…" She looks at me and then another weird thing happens—she smiles.

"Now," Principal Pootie says into the microphone for everyone to hear. "According to the rules, if a winner forfeits the prize, it automatically goes to the next in line, and that, my dear, is you."

"Are you kidding me?" I shriek. "Seriously?!"

"I'm keeping the tix to Disney, but yeah, you can have the whole London experience. I'm not really a building-schools, manual-labor kind of girl. You'll rock that challenge and make us all…proud."

And then she just steps off the podium and walks away.

"Can you believe that?" I say to Lucy, Lyric, and Stella Rose when I rush over to them.

"I guess we're all having moments of growth up in here today," Lyric says.

"You'll always be our queen," Stella Rose says, shutting off her camera. "What you just did up there was amazy. You showed us all that there are many different ways to win."

"Yeah," Lucy says. "A month ago you could barely get through your speech. That was a win right there."

I hold my finger in the air to clarify. "You mean I couldn't get through it at all."

"Who remembers a month ago anyway?" she jokes, chuckling with the rest of us. She's right, though. There's no need to look back unless you're checking to see how far you've come.

Lyric adds, "Our girl is going to London, all new and improved."

That's when I hear a voice behind me say, "You've always been a star. Your mom would be crying tears of joy today."

When I hear Lyric gasp, covering her mouth in shock, I whip around to see Jade Darby—right here at Valentine Middle, in our very own gymnasium.

"Ms. Darby!" I squeak as Lyric throws her arms around her mom.

"Mom." Lyric can barely get the words out of her mouth. "What...what're you doing here?"

"You know, Boogie," she says, pushing a curly tendril from her daughter's face, "I reread your email and decided that this is the only place I need to be right now."

"But don't you have shows? You're in the middle of your big tour."

"That can wait." She kisses Lyric's forehead, pulling her close, into her sequin-and-mesh top. "It can all wait."

"Thank you so much, Ms. Darby, for the post you made about Brookie's Cookies," I say to her, still completely stunned that I'm looking at her with my very own eyeballs.

"Something you said up there," she starts, nodding at the podium. "It really hit home for me."

"Something *I* said?"

"You're right. You *are* lucky to have each other, and I promise, Boogie, I'm going to do my best to be here for you, for all the big stuff, but for all the little stuff, too."

Lyric looks up to her mom with adoration.

"And yes, Brooklyn, you are already enough." She turns to Lyric and touches the tip of her nose. "And so are you, which means that no matter what song you pick—"

"You mean *we* pick, because now that you're here we're totally going to rock this audition selection," Lyric says, pulling her mom in one direction while Stella Rose pads off in the other.

Lucy and I watch Stella Rose ease into the bleachers and position the camera in front of her. She fidgets with her eyeglasses before unraveling her scarf. Then she smooths down its edges, sits up straight, and finally introduces herself to the documentary competition judges.

"Hi." She takes a deep breath and glances at me. I clasp my hands together and squeeze, nodding at her to do the same. I can't help but swell with hope when she imitates me right back. *You can do it*, I mouth at her.

She takes one long breath and goes for it. "My name is Stella Rose Sampson, and I'm submitting my documentary today in honor of one of my best friends, Brooklyn Ace. This is her story of redemption, of inspiration, of hope."

"Check out our girl," Lucy says, filming Stella Rose with her new camera phone.

I marvel at the way things are turning out. And Ms. Darby is right; Mom would be proud—of all of us.

"Brooklyn! Brooklyn!" the school reporter calls out to me. "Can I get a quote for my article?"

"Why would you want a quote from her?" Lucy snarks, shoving her hands into her hips. "You've been chasing a story about the cookie queen." Lucy nods at Piper Parker, who is soaking in her big win with her girls. "B's not the big winner after all."

301

"Oh, but she is," he says, looking around the gym at all the kids dancing to our hit song, which is playing on a loop.

"Sure, I'll give you a quote," I say, rocking back and forth on my feet. "I might not have won the big crown today, but for the record..." I hold my head high and watch Lyric and her mom checking out songs for her audition. Then I glance at Stella Rose, working through her video submission. Lucy snaps a pic of me with her phone, and I close my eyes and feel my mom right beside me before turning to the reporter to begin.

"I'm Brooklyn Ace, and it's my honor to be your Valentine Middle School cookie monster."

AUTHOR'S NOTE

Dear Reader,

You just finished reading about Brooklyn's experiences with grief and how she got the help she needed to manage it. Mental health is a very real and important issue that kids across the world are dealing with every day. Your feelings are valid. Always remember that you are a rock star, no matter the challenges in front of you. You were enough yesterday, you're enough today, and, that's right, you'll be enough tomorrow—even if it doesn't always feel like it. Just as Brooklyn discovers that it's perfectly okay not to be okay, I hope you'll always remember this, too. It's how we deal with the sticky "stuff" that matters most. On those days when the path feels too topsy-turvy to tread, I hope the special resources below will help. I picked them just for you.

I heart all these websites and books because they have helped so many kids get through tough times when a little extra support is needed—and we all need extra support from time to time. Asking for that help is your superpower to get back to your happy. And no matter what, you deserve it all!

Remember, you are loved! xo

From my heart to yours:

Websites:

National Alliance for Children's Grief:
childrengrieve.org

Black Mental Health Alliance: (410) 338-2642 /
blackmentalhealth.com

Therapy for Black Girls: therapyforblackgirls.com

Anxiety and Depression Association of America
(ADAA): adaa.org

Rainbows for all Children: rainbows.org

National Alliance on Mental Illness (NAMI):
nami.org

Books:

The Worry (Less) Book by Rachel Brian

Why Do I Feel So Sad? by Tracy Lambert-Prater

Where the Watermelons Grow by Cindy Baldwin

Genesis Begins Again by Alicia D. Williams

The Invisible String by Patrice Karst

The Invisible String Workbook by Patrice Karst

ACKNOWLEDGMENTS

Thank you, Timothy Shannon Johnson, the kinder and more patient person in this life partnership; you never stop holding me down. You rock for talking through all my little stories and for buying boxes of Thin Mints for me during cookie season.

Thank you to the dynamic team that keeps this middle-grade machine going. I have an incredible agent, Marcy Posner, who reads my words and continues to encourage my dreams with more love than I imagined possible.

My fab editors, Lisa Yoskowitz, Caitlyn Averett, and Hannah Milton, are pure geniuses. I appreciate your meticulous dedication to sparking life into the dream. You all get me, and you let me run wild on the pages creating Black joy. Thank you for being fearless captains on this mind-blowing ride.

And these book covers...*swoon*. They're dipped in some serious brilliance, thanks to Jenny Kimura and Yaoyao Ma Van As. Thank you for getting it right with my characters, who now, thanks to you, seem so very real to tons of girls who can see themselves represented beautifully and with so much style.

A special thank-you to the behind-the-scenes teams who work tirelessly for their authors. Marketing, Publicity, Sales, etc...., our girls get to discover and then lose themselves in our literary worlds because of you. Thank you!

Lastly, please know that my love is endless for all my friends and family, near and far, for continuing to encourage me—especially my Sisky, Kristy Goodwin, who breaks story with me like it's her night job.

P.S. Blondie, I'm finally out of your guest room, but my heart still dances because I know it will always have my name on it. I love you forever. And then forever again. And then, yeah...again.

We did it, girlfriend!